As Bill settled close to her on the richly upholstered leather seat, her heartbeat quickened.

The warning bells that should have been ringing all along finally went off in her head, but it was too late—much, much too late. They were alone together, shut off from the world, if only momentarily. And Mayor Harper—Bill—her former friend and lover, was taking her small hand and folding it into his much larger, warmer one.

"I haven't told you yet how good it is to see you again, have I, Eloise? Not just good, great," he said in the same soft, low utterly sexy voice that still sometimes haunted her dreams.

She knew she should offer him a snappy comeback, curt words cut with just the right amount of irony. Instead she clung to his hand, unable to stop herself from allowing her truest, deepest feelings to be revealed.

"It's good to see you again, too, Bill," she said at last. "Really, really good…"

Dear Reader,

As you ski into the holiday season, be sure to pick up the latest batch of Silhouette Special Edition romances. Featured this month is Annette Broadrick's latest miniseries, SECRET SISTERS, about family found after years of separation. The first book in this series is *Man in the Mist* (#1576), which Annette describes as "...definitely a challenge to write." About her main characters, Annette says, "Greg, the wounded lion hero—you know the type—gave me and the heroine a very hard time. But we refused to be intimidated and, well, you'll see what happened!"

You'll adore this month's READERS' RING pick, *A Little Bit Pregnant* (SE#1573), which is an emotional best-friends-turned-lovers tale by reader favorite Susan Mallery. *Her Montana Millionaire* (SE#1574) by Crystal Green is part of the popular series MONTANA MAVERICKS: THE KINGSLEYS. Here, a beautiful socialite dazzles the socks off a dashing single dad, but gets her own lesson in love. Nikki Benjamin brings us the exciting conclusion of the baby-focused miniseries MANHATTAN MULTIPLES, with *Prince of the City* (SE#1575). Two willful individuals, who were lovers in the past, have become bitter enemies. Will they find their way back to each other?

Peggy Webb tantalizes our romantic taste buds with *The Christmas Feast* (SE#1577), in which a young woman returns home for Christmas, but doesn't bargain on meeting a man who steals her heart. And don't miss *A Mother's Reflection* (SE#1578), Elissa Ambrose's powerful tale of finding long-lost family...and true love.

These six stories will enrich your hearts and add some spice to your holiday season. Next month, stay tuned for more page-turning and provocative romances from Silhouette Special Edition.

Happy reading!

Gail Chasan
Senior Editor

Please address questions and book requests to:
Silhouette Reader Service
U.S.: 3010 Walden Ave., P.O. Box 1325, Buffalo, NY 14269
Canadian: P.O. Box 609, Fort Erie, Ont. L2A 5X3

Prince of the City

NIKKI BENJAMIN

Silhouette®

SPECIAL EDITION™

Published by Silhouette Books

America's Publisher of Contemporary Romance

Special thanks and acknowledgment are given to Nikki Benjamin for her contribution to the MANHATTAN MULTIPLES series.

 SILHOUETTE BOOKS

ISBN 0-373-24575-0

PRINCE OF THE CITY

Visit Silhouette at www.eHarlequin.com

Printed in U.S.A.

NIKKI BENJAMIN

was born and raised in the Midwest, but after years in the Houston area, she considers herself a true Texan. Nikki says she's always been an avid reader. (Her earliest literary heroines were Nancy Drew, Trixie Belden and Beany Malone.) Her writing experience was limited, however, until a friend started penning a novel and encouraged Nikki to do the same. One scene led to another, and soon she was hooked.

**The exciting conclusion of
MANHATTAN MULTIPLES:**

*The doors of Manhattan Multiples might shut
down. The mayor and Eloise Vale once had
a thing. Someone on the staff is pregnant
and is keeping it a secret. Romance and
drama—and so many babies in the big city!*

Eloise Vale—As Manhattan Multiples'
director and the mother of triplet boys, she
finds enough to keep her busy. But her stomach
is in knots because of continuous threats from
a former flame, who is only the most powerful
man in the city!

Bill Harper—With an empire to rule, the
mayor of New York City has enough on his
mind without memories of Eloise Vale, the
only woman he's ever loved. And now she's
the enemy. Can he find a way to bridge the
gap between them?

Leah Simpson—This new mother has a
troubling past. Will danger follow her to
the doors of Manhattan Multiples?

Carl, Henry and John Vale—The terrible
triplet trio, as they've been dubbed by their
building's doorman. Of course, these thirteen-
year-olds are precious and want what's best
for their mother. They'll fight to ensure her
happiness, even if they have to go toe-to-toe
with the mayor of New York!

Chapter One

Eloise Vale paused in front of the mahogany-framed, full-length mirror in her bedroom one last time and cast a critical glance at her reflection.

The simple but elegant black silk gown skimming her ankles—scooped modestly at the neckline, but plunging low to bare her back—showed off her trim figure to best advantage. Her ash-blond hair swung full and smooth to the edge of her chin. Her makeup, applied just a bit more dramatically than usual, accentuated her features in a highly flattering manner. And her jewelry, limited to glittering diamond earrings and a matching diamond bracelet, added just the right touch of glamour.

Not bad for a mature woman of forty-two, and the mother of thirteen-year-old triplet sons, she thought, a wry smile tugging at the corners of her mouth. In fact, she looked cooler, calmer and more sophisticated than she felt, considering the public scrutiny she would be facing during the evening ahead.

Amazing how deceptive one's outward appearance—*her* outward appearance—could be, given the proper camouflage. And it was a darn good thing, too, under the circumstances. She couldn't allow herself the luxury of displaying in any way the heart-pounding anticipation that had been making her tummy flutter since midafternoon. Only then had she, finally, belatedly acknowledged that she might be about to open Pandora's box by attending the Mayor's Ball.

Going to New York City's premier social event of the fall season wasn't a new experience for Eloise. Before his death three years ago, her husband, Walter Vale, an affluent investment banker, had taken her to the ball regularly. Tonight, however, her escort would be the mayor himself, Bill Harper.

The man she had loved but refused to marry seventeen years ago. Also the man she had lately come to consider her nemesis.

"Something you would do well to remember," Eloise muttered, shaking a warning finger at her image in the mirror.

Bill Harper had proven the past few months that he was no friend of hers or Manhattan Multiples. He had only invited her to attend the ball with him because he wanted to look as if he was being fair-minded. And she had only accepted his invitation so she could use the occasion to *her* advantage.

The heated telephone calls she'd made to his office, the op-ed piece she'd written for the *New York Times* and the anonymous letters she'd written the editors of various other New York papers hadn't seemed to do the least bit of good. But maybe face-to-face, one-on-one, she could make some headway with him, and in the process garner additional public support for her cause.

Tilting her chin at a defiant angle, Eloise nodded once, strengthened by the memory of the pact she'd made with herself weeks ago. She was willing to do just about anything to save Manhattan Multiples, the nonprofit organization she'd started to benefit the mothers of multiple-birth babies. And if that included spending an entire evening in the spotlight as Mayor Harper's personal guest at the ball, then so be it.

She was smart and funny, and in the years she'd spent as the socialite wife of a prominent New York businessman, she had learned to be at ease in large gatherings. She could, and would, make the most of her appearance at tonight's event.

She also assumed Mayor Harper intended to do the same. She had no doubt that his reason for wanting to be seen with her that evening was purely political.

She wasn't naive enough to believe he had the slightest thought of picking up where they'd left off seventeen years ago. Neither had she, for that matter. Even though she was now a widow and he was divorced, her reasons for refusing his proposal of marriage were just as valid now as they had been then.

Certainly they had each changed in many ways over the years, but one deciding factor—*the* deciding factor when she'd turned down his proposal of marriage—still remained. Bill Harper was, and always would be, first and foremost, a politician.

And tonight he was only interested in using her as a means to deflect the criticism he'd received lately. Though popular with a good many people, his campaign to divert city funds from certain nonprofit organizations, including hers, and redirect them to renewing and revitalizing the city and its services across the board hadn't met with the kind of overwhelming support she knew he would like to garner from the city's population.

By being seen with her, and putting just the right spin on it, he could appear to have gained the cooperation of one of his more outspoken opponents. But Eloise also had a lot to gain. By being seen with the mayor, and putting just the right spin on it, *she* could make it seem as if he were considering her arguments supporting the maintenance of funding for the nonprofits in a favorable manner.

From past experience, she knew that polite public dialogue, aided and abetted by the proper spin, could work miracles. And as long as it *looked* as if she had the mayor's attention, there was a possibility that she could eventually rally enough support in favor of retaining city funding for nonprofit organizations, including Manhattan Multiples, to prevent significant and potentially ruinous cuts from being made.

Turning away from the mirror at last, Eloise quickly gathered her tiny black silk purse along with the ankle-length black silk coat that not only complemented her gown, but would also help to ward off the November chill in the night air. A last glance at the clock on the nightstand as she walked determinedly to the bedroom doorway assured her that she still had a few minutes remaining until her date was due to arrive.

No, not *date,* she reminded herself as her tummy fluttered nervously, yet again. That made the occasion seem more personal and potentially romantic than she was certain either Mayor Harper or she meant it to be. *Escort* was a much more dispassionate, and thus much more acceptable designation.

Her anxiety at least partially allayed, Eloise headed

down the hallway toward the living room, following the sound of raucous cheering, interspersed with masculine grunts and groans coming from the television set. She didn't dare look into her sons' bedroom doorways as she passed. Mrs. Kazinsky, her twice-weekly housekeeper, would be coming tomorrow.

Eloise had delegated all responsibility for maintaining some semblance of order in the boys' rooms to her, and she had to trust that the sturdy, gray-haired, no-nonsense woman would work her magic just as she always did during her visits to the penthouse apartment.

Pausing in the doorway of the long, wide, rectangular living room, Eloise checked the time again on the mantel clock over the fireplace that centered the more formal side of the room. There, also, two wing chairs and a love seat—elegantly upholstered but comfortable—framed a richly colored Persian rug.

Not quite five minutes more before she fully expected the doorbell to chime.

Bill Harper would be right on time, of course. He was punctuality personified. He had never kept her waiting. In fact, he had a reputation for never keeping anyone waiting, not the press or even the more vociferous of his rival politicians.

Eloise's gaze traveled on to the far end of the living room where a more casual grouping of overstuffed sofa and matching recliners surrounded a television set that was quite a bit larger than she considered absolutely necessary. Such a thing now having pride of place in her living room was a testament to what a pushover she could be where her sons were concerned.

Draped over the furniture in various stages of boyish slouch were her triplets. Boxes from the local pizza parlor, last seen in the kitchen, were now scattered on the glass and brass coffee table along with balled-up napkins, a gallon jug of milk and three empty glasses.

At least they'd used glasses, she thought with a rueful smile, a surge of love for her handsome, blond-haired boys warming her heart. They had been a handful since day one. They were also the main reason why she had started Manhattan Multiples. But she wouldn't have traded them for anything in the world. They had added more joy to her life than she had ever imagined she'd have.

"Yo, Mamma, looking good," Carl, the eldest by several minutes, called out. Apparently having dragged his attention from the wrestling match on TV, he hung his head back over the arm of one of the recliners and grinned at her impishly.

John, her middle son, the more serious expression on his face often distinguishing him from his brothers, rolled to his feet, vacating the other recliner. He surveyed her slowly from head to toe, them emitted a long, drawn-out wolf whistle that made her blush.

"Wow, Mom, you look really nice."

Henry, her youngest, scrambled off the sofa and demanded with a teasing grin all his own, "Who are you and what have you done with our real mother? She was last seen wearing baggy jeans and a grubby sweatshirt."

"Guys, give me a break, will you? You've seen me dressed in a ball gown, although I admit it's been a while," she reminded them, her prim tone of voice belied by her own gratified smile.

Passing muster with her sons never failed to boost her confidence. Not that they were overly critical. They were, however, always brutally frank. Had they not liked her attire, they would have been equally outspoken, a trait she had long since learned to appreciate as well-meaning.

"It *has* been a while. And you've never gone out on a date with some strange guy, either," Carl replied, taking on the protective role of eldest son.

"It isn't a date, at least not a *real* date. It's actually more of a…business meeting. We're just conducting it at a party rather than at the office. And Bill Harper isn't a stranger. He's the mayor of New York City and he's also an old friend of mine," Eloise advised before she had time to remember she hadn't previously mentioned *that* fact to her sons.

"An old friend?" John frowned ominously, the designated worrier.

Obviously he had assumed they already knew all of her friends, old as well as new.

"Aha, the plot thickens," Henry chortled, rubbing his hands together in gleeful anticipation of the possibility for future bedevilment. "Mom and the mayor…once old friends, now sworn enemies."

"We are not enemies, sworn or otherwise. We simply have opposing viewpoints on several issues," Eloise explained patiently.

"So you're actually only…adversaries." Carl eyed her smugly, showing off his prep school education to best advantage.

"Yeah, Carl," John joined in. "Mom and the mayor are *only* adversaries."

"Poor guy…he doesn't stand a chance, does he?" Henry asked.

"Not with our mom as an *adversary*," Carl replied.

The doorbell chimed loudly, not only startling them all, but also, thankfully, cutting off any further discussion of her relationship with Bill Harper.

Shooting her sons a warning look, Eloise crossed to the intercom, exchanged greetings with the doorman, who announced Mayor Harper's arrival, then instructed him to send the mayor up to her apartment.

In an effort to quell the sudden reoccurrence of the butterflies in her stomach, she then turned back to her sons. All of them now hovered a few feet away, the wrestling match they'd been watching on the television totally forgotten.

"Need I ask you to *please* behave yourselves and mind your manners?"

"No, ma'am," they replied in unison.

Though their faces were solemn, their bright blue eyes twinkled mischievously.

"Have all of you finished your homework?"

"Yes, ma'am."

"Can I trust you to clean up the living room before you go to bed?"

"Yes, ma'am."

"Bed by ten o'clock at the latest, okay? You know you have school tomorrow."

"Ah, Mom—"

A sharp rap of the brass doorknocker interrupted any further argument her sons were about to give. They looked at each other, though, and then they looked at Eloise, each of them offering her an identical teasing grin.

"Mom, the door," Carl prompted when she continued to stand and stare at them, her heart suddenly pounding, her purse and her coat gripped tightly in her hands.

"Yeah, Mom, the door," Henry urged.

"Want me to get it?" John took a step forward.

"I'll get it," she said, her voice sounding odd—almost breathy—to her own ears.

She crossed the living room to the small foyer slowly, the boys naturally trailing along in her wake.

"Hey, he's just an old friend with an opposing viewpoint," Carl reminded her kindly when she hesitated a long moment, her hand clasping the brass doorknob.

"Right," she muttered casting him a grateful smile.

"You look great, Mom," Henry said, giving her shoulder a reassuring pat.

"And you're smart, too," John added for good measure.

Also just the tiniest bit terrified of what's waiting for me on the other side of my front door, Eloise added silently, for her benefit alone. Then, drawing a steadying breath, she turned the bolt lock decisively.

She opened the door with a welcoming whoosh, then stood absolutely still, staring at Bill Harper with a barely contained gasp of astonishment.

She had thought she had been prepared to meet him again face-to-face for the first time in seventeen years. She had seen his picture in the paper often enough, as well as his image on the television screen. But he had been removed to a sure and certain distance on those occasions.

The lines and angles that made his face so appealingly attractive, the vitality in his bright blue eyes, the power and strength of his long, lithe frame had always been muted. Lounging casually on her doorstep, as he now was, elegantly dressed in a black tuxedo, his short salt-and-pepper hair neatly combed, his gaze direct, the smile tugging at the corners of his mouth warm and gracious, he was downright devastating, as were the memories that all too suddenly flooded through her.

As Eloise continued to meet his steady gaze, the years seemed to melt away under a rush of warmth edged with a longing that caught her completely by surprise. In those first few moments, she could think of him only as her old friend, her once dearest, most beloved friend—the man she could have married, would have married…if only. And she imagined, for the space of a heartbeat, how wonderful it would be to step into his arms that very moment, to hold him close and be held, in turn, by him.

Then, remembering that her sons stood right behind her, taking in the scene, no doubt much more avidly that she would have liked, Eloise gave herself a firm mental shake. Bill Harper had been her friend once, emphasis on *had been.* Now, as Carl had so nicely put it, he was her adversary. And as such, he threatened everything she had worked for with a fund-cutting flourish of his mayoral pen.

"Mr. Mayor," she greeted him politely, offering her hand along with a dignified smile. "Come in, please, and let me introduce you to my sons."

"Please, Eloise, call me Bill," he replied, his tone equally polite.

He wrapped her hand in both of his far larger and much warmer ones, then held on to it just a tad longer than absolutely necessary, his blue eyes sparkling just as devilishly as her sons' eyes had earlier.

"Of course…Bill." She felt her cheeks warm as she finally managed to pull her hand free. Gesturing to each of her sons in turn, she added, "Carl, John and Henry."

"Mr. Mayor, nice to meet you," each said as he shook hands with them, showing the same warmth he'd shown her.

"Boys, nice to meet all of you, too." He glanced at Eloise, his tone suddenly teasing as he added, "How on earth do you tell them apart?"

"It's not always easy," she admitted with a wry smile. "But I have my ways."

"I'll bet you do," Bill said, his smile widening. "She's not easy to fool, is she?" He directed the question to her sons.

"No, sir, not at all," Carl replied as John and Henry exchanged amused glances.

"It's good to know some things never change." Bill favored Eloise with a look that struck her as all too familiar, not to mention much too knowing. Then he glanced at his heavy gold watch, the only jewelry he wore. "I suppose we'd better go. We don't want to keep my constituents waiting, do we?"

"Not tonight," she agreed, trying, unsuccessfully, to ignore her nervousness.

"Why don't you let me help you with your coat?" Reaching out, Bill took it from her.

"Yes, of course. Thank you."

Eloise glanced up at him again, and her cheeks warmed even more at the intensity still evident in his eyes, still plainly directed her way. Turning, she slid her arms into the silken sleeves of her coat as he held it open for her. As she fumbled with the rhinestone buttons, her fingers refusing to work properly, he put his hands on her shoulders and squeezed gently as if to reassure her in some way. The deft flex of his fingers through the fabric of her coat was not only heartening, but also disturbingly distracting.

Startled by an unexpected wave of heat that welled up deep within her, Eloise cast another wordless glance at Bill. His smile now had a mischievous hint to it, making her realize—as he must—just how easily she could once again become putty in his all-too-clever hands.

Taking a firm grip on her rioting emotions, and a decisive step away from the mayor, Eloise directed a stern look at each of her sons in turn.

"Bed by ten," she reminded them.

"Yes, ma'am," they chorused.

"I have my pager in my purse in case you need me for any reason."

"We won't," Carl assured her.

"I doubt I'll be out all that late," she added.

Though she couldn't say for sure, Eloise didn't think Bill would want to spend any more time with her than absolutely necessary, especially once he'd attained maximum benefit from the photo ops attendant upon their being seen together in public. And, of course, she had no desire to linger in his company, either.

"You'd better not, Mom. You have to go to work tomorrow, and we all know how cranky you can be when you don't get a good night's sleep," John admonished, his expression mockingly stern.

"Ah, so the lady still has to have a full eight hours of sleep to function," Bill said, more than a hint of laughter lacing his voice. "I'll be sure to keep that in mind."

Exchanging what appeared to be conspiratorial glances with her sons, Bill shook hands again with each of them, then opened the door and gestured with a stately flourish.

"Eloise…"

Feeling just the slightest bit at a disadvantage, she lifted her chin, forced herself to meet his gaze and attempted a haughty smile as she stepped into the hallway.

"Thank you, Bill."

She couldn't think how she had expected the evening to unfold, but she was fairly certain she had already lost most, if not all control of the situation, and they weren't even out of her apartment building yet. She also knew she should be trying to eliminate what seemed like a serious disadvantage on her part. But oddly enough, she couldn't seem to get motivated in that particular direction.

Not when Bill took her arm and escorted her onto the elevator. Not as they rode down to the lobby in silence, his presence beside her comfortingly familiar. Not when the doorman greeted them politely, and not when the driver did likewise as he opened the door of the long, black limousine for them.

Only as Bill settled close to her on the richly upholstered leather seat and the door closed with a solid thunk, sealing them into luxurious privacy did her heartbeat quicken. The warning bells that should have been ringing all along finally went off in her head, but it was too late—much, much too late. They were alone together, shut off from the world, if only momentarily. And Mayor Harper—Bill Harper—her former friend and lover, and now the perpetrator of the possible undoing of all she'd worked so hard to achieve the past twelve years, was reaching out, taking her small, cold hand and folding it into his much larger, warmer one.

"I haven't told you yet how good it is to see you again, have I, Eloise? And it *is* good to see you, finally face-to-face. Not just good, *great,* really, really *great…*" he said in the same soft, low, utterly sexy voice that still sometimes haunted her dreams.

She knew she should offer him a snappy comeback, curt words cut with just the right amount of irony. Instead she clung to his hand unabashedly, unable to stop herself from allowing her truest, deepest feelings to be revealed. She had loved Bill Harper once, and that love had never completely died. To pretend that it had, no matter how important the reason, was something she was simply too honest to do.

"It's good to see you again, too, Bill," she said at last. "Really, really good…"

Chapter Two

Until the moment Eloise Vale looked up at him in the limousine and admitted she was glad to see him again, Bill Harper had been gliding uncomfortably on the edge of uncertainty.

Seventeen years had passed since she'd turned down his proposal of marriage. He hadn't allowed himself to believe that she'd retained any but the most pragmatic feelings for him during the time they'd spent living their separate lives. And her outspoken, unabashedly negative opinion of his proposed cuts to city funding had made it all too possible that her behavior toward him might be downright hostile.

Bill couldn't say for sure exactly what had motivated him to ask Eloise to accompany him to the Mayor's Ball as his personal guest. In fact, he had debated for weeks whether or not to do it.

But some force deep inside him had warned with ever-increasing urgency that renewing his old acquaintance with Eloise—his beloved Eloise—was fast becoming a now-or-never proposition.

He hadn't wanted her to continue thinking of him as an enemy, as she would have so easily been able to do at a distance. At the very least, he had wanted to find some way for her to be able to consider him a friend.

Though, in all honesty, he wanted more than friendship from her, so much more. And he had known, intuitively, that if he expected to have any chance of winning back her affection, he had to act without further delay, or live to regret it the rest of his life.

He had finally issued his invitation—not by telephone but by handwritten note—fully anticipating that Eloise would politely refuse. Instead, she had accepted via a graciously worded, handwritten note of her own.

Bill had reread that note daily during the two weeks since he'd received it—two very long weeks when he had also contemplated every possible reason why she might decide to bow out at the last minute. She hadn't, of course. And, in fact, he should have known all along that she wouldn't.

Eloise Vale had always been as good as her word, something Bill knew well from firsthand experience. She had honored her promise to marry Walter Vale seventeen years ago, hadn't she? And though her decision had been a painful one for him to bear, Bill had admired her loyalty then as he did now, even knowing that tonight she was only there with him out of dedication to Manhattan Multiples.

He had been fully aware, as certain members of his staff had taken great pains to point out, that she could, and most likely would, use her attendance at the Mayor's Ball as his personal guest to the advantage of her nonprofit organization. But as he sat beside Eloise on the limousine's plush leather seat, breathing in the light, fresh scent of her perfume, he saw the warmth in her pale-gray eyes as she met his gaze, and he knew that she really was happy to see him again. As happy as he was to see her, though she hadn't sounded quite convinced as she'd said the words.

She was much too forthright to dissemble. And although her behavior toward him since his arrival at her apartment had been somewhat reserved, he had most certainly detected an underlying cordiality in her demeanor. He had seen the sparkle of anticipation in her eyes, the same anticipation he had felt as they'd met each other's gaze for the first time in too many years. And he had known that it had nothing to do with causes to be won. . The source of Eloise's inner excitement was much more personal, and thus much more heartening than Bill had dared to hope.

"May I say that you look lovely tonight?" he asked.

Finally feeling sure of himself and the rightness of his decision to renew his personal acquaintance with her again, Bill determined to take full advantage of the short, very private ride to the hotel where the ball was being held. He wanted to set aside, as much as he possibly could, all thoughts of the current conflict between them, and he wanted Eloise to do the same.

Inconceivable as he knew it would likely prove to be under the circumstances, he wanted them to be two ordinary people, a man and a woman, enjoying each other's company as they got to know each other again. And he wanted to believe Eloise, too, had felt a jolt of electric attraction similar to the one he'd experienced when he'd helped her into the black silk coat that complemented her dress so well.

"Only if you mean it," she replied with a wry smile, her tone not the least bit coy.

"I wouldn't have said it otherwise."

"Thank you." She looked down a moment, seeming shy all of a sudden, then glanced at him again, still smiling, her voice teasing as she added, "You look awfully nice yourself, Mr. Mayor. Very elegant, not to mention quite distinguished…"

"I appreciate the compliment, Eloise, but you don't have to be so formal," he admonished gently, unwilling to allow her to erect even that small barrier between them.

"Actually, I think I should, all things considered." Though she still smiled up at him, she now did so with a slight, seemingly defensive tip of her chin. "And you've more than earned the title," she added. "There's no reason why you shouldn't enjoy it."

"While I can?"

"Your words, not mine."

Eloise's eyes flashed with a teasing gleam that brought back such a rush of memories Bill's breath caught in his throat. He had forgotten what an excellent sparring partner she could be—bright and quick and full of humor. And remembering, he recalled, as well, that it had often been necessary to kiss her senseless in order to put an end to their verbal battles.

Much as he liked the idea, he didn't dare do that now, though. He could, however, attempt to change the subject.

"Meant facetiously, of course."

"Of course," she agreed without any obvious sign of conviction.

"I enjoyed meeting your sons. You must be very proud of them, and rightly so."

"I am—very, *very* proud. They can be a handful at times, and of course, they have only just entered their teens so I expect I'm going to have quite a few challenges to face, especially over the next couple of years. They don't gang up on me nearly as much as they could. Still, I'm trying to prepare myself for whatever rocky times lie ahead. They're basically good kids, though. And they seem to understand, more often than not, how much I've come to depend on their cooperation since their father's death."

"I was really sorry to hear about Walter."

"Losing him the way we did was hard on all of us," Eloise admitted. "He had always been in such good health and he'd just had a complete physical. The doctor assured me that the results of all the tests had been negative. They'd had no reason to suspect he might have a massive heart attack, and no way of foreseeing the possibility, either."

"I wish I could have been here for the funeral," Bill said, recalling how helpless he'd felt, stuck in a snowstorm in upstate New York, the one time he might have been of some help to her. "But I didn't hear about his death until it was too late to get back to the city."

"The flowers you sent were beautiful, and your card meant so much to me, too." She hesitated a moment, looking away. "Walter always thought a lot of you. He always admired all of your hard work, too."

"I always thought a lot of Walter, as well. And you, Eloise…"

Tentatively he took her hand in his and gave it a gentle squeeze. To his surprise and gratification, she didn't pull away immediately, but held on to him as if grateful, as well, for the physical contact he had finally taken the chance of initiating.

"You've had your ups and downs, too," she said after a few moments, glancing up at him again. "I was sorry to read about your divorce from Marnie Hartwell."

"She's a wonderful woman, very happily remarried with a third baby on the way. We had some good times together, but unfortunately, we had different priorities—something we refused to admit until after we'd married. At least our parting was not only mutually agreeable, but also amicable. Or as mutually agreeable and amicable as that kind of parting can be."

There had been so much more to his rebound marriage and subsequent divorce than his simple statements indicated. But there wasn't enough time now to give Eloise more than the sanitized version generally put out for public consumption. Not that he or Marnie had any deep, dark secrets to hide, but one day he hoped to be able to tell Eloise the whole truth about why his perfectly good marriage had ultimately failed.

"And you've been a confirmed bachelor ever since," she said, now gazing at him with an assessing look, one eyebrow quizzically raised. "Although you always seem to have an attractive woman on your arm whenever you attend an event of any great importance."

"Keeping tabs on my social life, are you, Eloise? I'm flattered."

"Well, there's absolutely no reason at all for you to be. Your picture is in all of the papers all of the time. Everyone in the entire city can keep tabs on your social life whether they want to or not."

"True enough, but then I am the mayor." He gave her hand another squeeze as the limousine pulled to the curb in front of the Waldorf Astoria Hotel and the milling photographers awaiting his arrival eyed the vehicle with sudden interest. "And tonight I have the most attractive woman I've ever known on my arm. I can't even begin to tell you how proud and how happy that makes me feel.''

Taking advantage of Eloise's momentarily stunned silence, he bent and kissed her lightly on the cheek. Then, as the driver exited the limousine, he flashed her an encouraging smile.

''Ms. Vale, it's an honor to have you here with me tonight.''

''I bet you say that to all the ladies, Mr. Mayor,'' she retorted in a wry tone, obviously having collected herself once again.

''Never once, to anyone else, Eloise. I swear.''

''Thank you, then…Mr. Mayor.''

He slanted a disappointed look at her, but she met his gaze unwaveringly, her demeanor cool and calm as she clung righteously to what was really nothing more than a mere thread of formality. Tonight he wanted her to think of him only as Bill Harper, but he couldn't really blame her for choosing not to. They might have a history together, an intimate history filled with many, many pleasant memories. But here and now they were on opposite sides of a very important political fence, and they both had a lot at stake.

He knew that Eloise was no more likely to be bulldozed into changing her stance than he was. But he had no intention of doing anything like that tonight. Surprisingly enough, he had no hidden agenda at all for the evening ahead. He wanted only to enjoy the pleasure of her company. And he sincerely hoped that she would be able to enjoy his company, as well.

''Okay, have it your way,'' he relented with a grin as the driver opened the rear door of the limousine.

She rewarded him with another of her wry smiles.

"I could be so lucky."

"Well, you have to roll the dice first," he advised. "Ready?"

"As ready as I'll ever be," she replied, keeping a hold on his hand as he helped her out of the limousine amid the sudden click and flash of cameras aimed at them from all directions.

So much for private time, Bill thought as he paused on the sidewalk outside the hotel, put an arm around Eloise's shoulders, drew her close to his side and smiled graciously for the hoard of hardworking photographers. Standing next to him, Eloise seemed equally at ease in the limelight, her own smile dazzling, subtly reminding him that she was a powerful force in her own right— one with which he would eventually have to reckon.

Not tonight, though, he determined. Tonight he planned to do everything in *his* substantial power to see that Eloise Vale had the time of her life as his very special guest at this very special party held in his honor.

Eloise couldn't remember ever having quite as much *fun* at a social engagement as she had at the Mayor's Ball that night. She had attended many, many similar high-society events in the past with much higher expectations of enjoyment, only to be sadly disappointed. And since she had agreed to accompany Bill Harper to the Mayor's Ball solely as a means of promoting her cause—the continuation of city funding for nonprofit organizations including her own Manhattan Multiples— she had known better than to also count on having a good time.

As she had on every other occasion when she'd felt duty-bound to attend a particular event, she had wanted only to be able to get through the ordeal with as much grace and charm as she could muster. But from the moment she had opened her apartment door to Mayor Harper, a whole new world filled with surprising possibilities seemed to open up for her, as well—not only for the evening ahead, but for the very near future, too.

He was so relaxed in her presence, and they had so many shared memories—truly fond memories—that her attempts to maintain some semblance of formality between them seemed more and more ludicrous as the night wore on. And the longer she was with Bill Harper, the harder it was for her to think of him as an adversary, until finally, reluctantly, she gave up on it altogether.

He gave every appearance of being genuinely proud to have her by his side, pausing outside the hotel, and again inside the grand ballroom, to allow the photographers on hand to duly record their presence there together. Granted, he would benefit from the exposure, but so would she. Nor was she cynical enough to assume his high spirits were due only, or even mainly, to any possible gain in political advantage he might make at her expense. Public opinion could be swayed just as easily in the direction of her cause, as he must surely know.

Once swept up in the glamour and excitement of the Mayor's Ball, Eloise wasn't able to allow serious thoughts to distract her for very long. Even though saving city funding for Manhattan Multiples remained a very real problem that nagged at the back of her mind throughout the evening, she was too busy enjoying Bill's attentive company to focus on it as completely as she probably should have. And while that could have been exactly what Bill intended, he seemed to be having just as much fun as she was, something even *he* couldn't fake for very long.

After seeing to it that her black silk coat was safely

stowed away, he snagged a glass of champagne for each of them off a passing waiter's tray. Then he took her on a tour of the ballroom, filled to near capacity with the city's most important men and women, movers and shakers one and all, dressed in their finest and eager to make their presence as well as their various positions known to the mayor. Bill greeted them all with equal affability, also making sure to introduce Eloise.

His very dear friend, he said over and over again, smiling at her with such obvious warmth that he not only made her heart glow, but also made her believe it was true.

Some people eyed them with obvious surprise while others seemed somewhat dismayed. But most responded to them with a nonchalance that put her even more at ease.

It *was* possible, after all, for two people with very differing opinions to be friends. And though not widely known among their contemporaries, she and Bill *had* had a close personal relationship long before their conflict over city funding had arisen.

Having completed his meet-and-greet duties, Bill lured Eloise to the buffet table and piled a white china plate high with tantalizing tidbits for them to share. Then he led her off to a secluded alcove where a table for two—complete with white linen tablecloth and a centerpiece of pale pink roses—had been discreetly tucked away, reserved just for them, obviously at his special request.

"This is lovely," Eloise said as he seated her in one of the fabric-draped chairs. "But how did you manage it?"

"Well, I *am* the mayor," he reminded her—as he seemed to enjoy doing—his tone teasing.

"And the center of attention at your very own ball, as well you should be. I didn't think hiding out in a private nook was allowed at an affair of this magnitude, though."

Unselfconsciously, Eloise helped herself to a miniature quiche that proved to be simply delicious.

"Even the mayor of New York City needs an occasional respite. Or maybe I should say *especially* the mayor." Bill, too, helped himself to one of the morsels he had selected from the buffet. "I imagine you've often felt the same way, sponsoring as many fund-raising events as you do."

"There are a lot of times when I'd much rather be home alone, wearing my baggiest sweats, curled up on the sofa with a good book and a cup of tea," she admitted. "But smiling and shaking hands and making small talk with strangers at yet another function for yet another good cause has become more and more of a necessity lately."

"I hope tonight isn't one of those times you'd rather be home," he said, his concern for her feelings evident.

"No, not tonight," she replied, not only unable, but also unwilling to hide her true feelings from him. "Tonight, much to my surprise, I'm actually having a very good time."

"You know, so am I," Bill admitted, sounding just the slightest bit surprised himself. Then he added with a wicked grin, "I can't remember when that happened last. Must be the company we're keeping, huh?"

"Must be," Eloise agreed, smiling as well, as she snitched the last appetizer from the plate on the table.

"Have you had enough to eat or would you like me to make another foray to the buffet table?"

"Enough for now, although you could probably tempt

me with something decadently rich and sweet from the dessert table a little later.''

"How about a dance then?" Bill suggested as the orchestra began playing a soft, sexy ballad that had always been one of her favorites.

"A dance would be nice," Eloise agreed, remembering a long-ago night when they had held each other close, swaying to a similarly slow rhythm in a smoky club somewhere in Greenwich Village—a world away from the ballroom at the Waldorf Astoria.

"It's been a while," he said quietly, seeming to recall, as well, their last dance together as he stood to help her from her chair.

"I've been told dancing is like riding a bike," she quipped as he took her hand, wanting to recapture the lighthearted mood they'd been sharing. "Once you learn, you never forget."

"There are a lot of things I've never forgotten, Eloise," Bill murmured as they reached the dance floor and he took her in his arms. "Holding you like this is definitely at the top of the list."

Her heart fluttering, Eloise leaned against Bill wordlessly as he guided her into a simple box step. She had never forgotten completely the feel of his arms around her, either, even though there had been times when she had tried desperately to do so.

And now, as his long, lean, masculine frame seemed to curve protectively around her shorter, slighter self, the heat of his body melding with hers, she breathed in the fresh, clean scent of his aftershave and experienced a sense of peace and happiness she hadn't known she'd been missing.

It felt so good, so *right,* to be held in Bill Harper's arms. And though she knew these moments she shared with him were fleeting, she closed her eyes and pretended they would last forever.

As the music played on, one song segueing into another, he didn't speak and gratefully neither did she. The spell would be broken soon enough without any help from her. The orchestra cooperated a little longer, playing a third slow and easy ballad, then finally picked up the tempo by several beats with an old disco favorite.

"I'm still not much good at the faster dance steps," Bill admitted with obvious regret.

"Neither am I," Eloise said.

Taking his cue, she stepped out of his arms, but didn't pull her hand away when he seemed inclined to hold on to it.

"How about another glass of champagne?" he asked as he led her off the dance floor. "Or maybe something from the dessert table?"

Before Eloise could reply, they were waylaid by an investment banker who had been an associate of her husband's, and his bejeweled wife. While Eloise spoke to them, Bill flagged down a waiter and got them each another glass of champagne. Then they seemed to be swept up in another round of pressing the flesh as late arrivals sought to make their presence known to the ball's guest of honor and his lovely companion.

To his credit, Bill made sure they passed by the long, linen-covered table filled with desserts. Acknowledging in a teasing tone his recollection of her notorious taste for sweets, he helped her select a sampling of the luscious pastries on offer there.

But they weren't able to slip away alone again. Instead, they were invited to sit at a large round table full of corporate leaders, an invitation Eloise knew they were both wise to graciously accept.

These were the men and women most likely to support nonprofit organizations like Manhattan Multiples. Of course, they were also just as likely to support major cuts in city funding, especially if it meant there wouldn't be any increase in corporate taxes as a result, Eloise reminded herself as she nibbled on a tiny slice of sinfully delicious chocolate cake. Thankfully, no one at the table was boorish enough to bring up the subject, though.

But Eloise sensed an avid interest among their table mates in her rather odd and obviously unexpected appearance at the ball as Mayor Harper's special guest when everyone knew they held opposing views on such an important and potentially volatile issue. She should really be much more concerned about what people thought, Eloise admitted. But she was feeling so mellow that it was easier to just drift along, nodding and smiling and occasionally offering an appropriate, if inane, comment whenever necessary.

"How about a last dance…for tonight?" Bill asked as the conversation around them fell into a lull and the orchestra once again slowed the tempo of the music.

"Yes, please."

The rhythm of her heart quickening once again, Eloise smiled at him graciously, ignoring as best she could the raised eyebrows of several of the women as she took his proffered hand. She hadn't missed Bill's "for tonight," and apparently, neither had they. But she knew better than they that he was only trying to charm her.

Under the circumstances, they wouldn't be spending any more time together after tonight unless one or the other of them changed their political position. And that was highly unlikely to happen.

"Excuse us, everyone," Bill said, and whisked her

onto the dance floor as if afraid she would change her mind.

Fat chance of that happening, either, Eloise thought, as she stepped into his open arms and allowed herself to be enfolded in his masculine embrace one last time.

"I hope you didn't mind my dragging you off the way I did, but it's getting late and I wanted to dance with you again before we left," Bill admitted somewhat sheepishly.

"I didn't mind at all," Eloise assured him, smiling as she met his questing gaze.

"Good."

He drew her closer, his arms tightening around her imperceptibly as he brushed his cheek against her hair.

As the music played on, Eloise had a good idea of exactly how Cinderella must have felt, the clock ticking away the moments until she would be dropped back into the real world again. Her party was about to be over very soon, too. And in the morning she would once again have to face her own version of the real world, along with the very real problems she had come no closer to solving that night.

She had spent several hours with Mayor Harper, and although most of that time had also been spent with other people, as well, she'd had more than one opportunity to broach the subject of his proposed cuts to city funding. But she hadn't done it, and she wasn't going to.

Not as they danced together one last time, and not on the short ride back to her apartment, sitting close beside him in the privacy of his black limousine, the bright lights of the city muted by the tinted glass in the windows.

Certainly she was entitled to a little downtime, she

reasoned justifiably. And certainly she was entitled to spend that downtime in harmony with an old and very dear friend, renewing an acquaintance that would be of benefit to her and, by association, to Manhattan Multiples, as well.

Or so she tried to believe as she tucked her head against Bill's shoulder and allowed her hand to remain firmly clasped in his.

Whatever differences they had—and there were some—could, and would, be addressed. But at another time, in another place, she vowed, aware of how fleeting peaceful moments like the ones they now shared had lately seemed to be in her normally hectic life.

Bill appeared to be no more inclined to talk than she was, either in the limousine or on the all too speedy elevator ride to her apartment, though he did seem to want to keep ahold of her hand. Eloise was grateful on both counts. Tonight had been a very special night for her, one she would never forget. But just like Cinderella, she knew the countdown to its end would be over very soon now.

"I had a really good time tonight," Bill said as the elevator door whispered open on her floor.

Stepping off together, they started slowly down the hallway, the plush carpet muffling their footsteps, the pale glow of the art deco wall sconces lighting their way.

"So did I," Eloise replied, risking a glance at him as they came to a halt just outside her apartment door.

She knew immediately that she had made a big mistake by meeting his gaze. Knew, too, what was coming next and that she had a duty to discourage it. But the look of longing in Bill's bright blue eyes, edged with just the right hint of masculine mischief, made it impossible for her to do anything quite so sensible.

She was capable only of standing silently, caught and held by his mesmerizing gaze, as she awaited the inevitable and not unwelcome moment they had been moving toward all evening.

"I'm so glad we finally got together again," he continued, his voice pitched a notch lower.

Obviously feeling much too sure of himself, he offered her another winning smile.

"Yes," she agreed, brought back to earth again by his show of confidence. "I'm glad, too." Then, gathering her wits about her as she should have done much sooner, she ever so politely extended her hand. "Thank you for a lovely evening, Bill."

"Thank *you,* Eloise," he replied, his smile widening. "For making it much more than a lovely evening."

Pulling her close before she could even think of resisting, he bent his head and gently, chastely claimed her lips with his.

Eloise had forgotten how gratifying even the simplest kiss could be, especially when shared with someone as desirable as Bill Harper had always been to her.

It wasn't as if thoughts of him had ever interfered with her marital happiness, and it certainly wasn't as if she had ever obsessed about him sexually. But Bill had meant so much to her once upon a time.

So surely it wasn't odd that her attraction to him had lingered over time, tucked away in the far reaches of her fondest-days-past memories. Nor was it any surprise at all that she found herself responding to his kiss with an ardor that she would have never displayed with any other man, even though some reticence on her part probably would have been wise.

But she didn't want to be wise tonight, Eloise decided as Bill deepened their kiss ever so slightly.

Tracing the line of her lips with a teasing tongue, he sought entry, finding it as she uttered a soft sigh, relaxed against him and teased back with her own tongue.

His arms tightened around her possessively as they tasted each other intimately, and she sighed again, raising up on her toes, seeking desperately to get as close to him as she could. She wanted to feel even more completely the warmth radiating so seductively from his body—wanted, secretly, to dispense with all the clothing keeping her from putting her hands and her mouth against his hot, bare skin.

Suddenly, somewhere much too close to them, a door opened with a heavy rush. The sound registered in Eloise's mind, along with the faintest hint of boyish snickering, setting off a vague sense of alarm. But she was too enthralled by Bill's sensual kiss to react as promptly or appropriately as she should have. And then it was too late. She was thoroughly and completely caught in the act by her sons.

"Hey, Mom," Henry, the youngest, sang out. "You're late."

"Yeah, Mom, you are *way* late," John, her middle son, chided. "Way, way, *way* late. We expected you to be home *hours* ago."

"Do you know how worried we've been?" Carl, the eldest, demanded, his tone resembling one she had often used herself with them, only without the obvious touch of humor blended in for good measure. "I'm here to tell you that you are *so* grounded."

"Yeah, *so* grounded, Mom," Henry and John echoed, barely able to contain their laughter.

Totally flustered, Eloise took a step back as Bill broke off their kiss with a masculine chuckle.

"Looks like we have an audience," he muttered, his blue eyes gleaming with what appeared to be pride.

Though he shifted to one side so that he faced her sons—all three crowded into the open doorway of the apartment—he still kept a possessive arm around her shoulders.

"Sorry, guys, it's my fault your mom's late getting home. We were having so much fun together we lost all track of time."

"A likely story," Carl retorted grimly, but his eyes twinkled, too, as did his brothers'.

"You three were supposed to be in bed no later than ten o'clock," Eloise reminded them primly, going on the offensive.

They looked so cute in the red plaid flannel pants and red long-sleeved T-shirts they had recently adopted in lieu of pajamas that she wanted to hug them. But *they* were the ones who were up much too late tonight—a school night—against her expressed wishes.

"And a good thing we weren't," John replied severely. "Otherwise, who knows what you might have gotten yourself into out here in the hallway?"

"Yeah, Mom, who knows?" Henry added.

"She's safe with me," Bill assured them. "Although I must admit I couldn't resist snatching one little kiss before I said good-night." He traded conspiratorial grins with her sons then transferred his charming gaze back to Eloise. "Thank you for a wonderful evening, Ms. Vale."

"You're welcome, Mr. Mayor," she murmured in reply, not quite able to look him in the eye.

Bending, Bill gave her a last quick kiss on the cheek, and added very quietly for her ears only, "I'll call you," as he gave her shoulder a gentle, reassuring squeeze.

Then, to her sons, he saluted smartly.

"Gentlemen, don't be too hard on her."

"We won't," Carl answered for all of them.

"And don't you be too hard on them," he instructed Eloise, his grin widening for an instant before he turned and headed down the hallway to the elevator.

"Yeah, Mom, don't be too hard on us," Henry pleaded in a teasing tone as she made herding gestures with her hands to get them out of the hallway and back inside the apartment where they belonged.

"We were only looking out for you, Mom," John reminded her.

"'Cause we love you," Carl added wisely.

"You are never going to be able to get out of bed in the morning, much less be able to stay awake all day," she chastised them. "I'm not paying good money to a private school for you to fall asleep in class."

"Hey, it's already morning. Maybe we should just stay up," Henry suggested.

"Absolutely not. You are all going to bed without any further delay, and I don't want to hear a single complaint from any of you when your alarms go off at six o'clock."

"Like you're even going to be up then yourself," Carl quipped as he headed into his room.

"Oh, I'll be up," Eloise vowed, remembering the busy day she had ahead of her. Then remembering, too, that she hadn't done anything tonight to alleviate any of the problems awaiting resolution at Manhattan Multiples, she added by way of warning, "And I'll also be just a little cranky."

"No, please, not Cranky Mom," Henry teased as he scurried into his room.

''A fate worse than death,'' John said, peeling off down the hallway into his room, as well.

''Good night, boys,'' Eloise called out, smiling to herself as she continued on to her bedroom.

''Good night, Mom,'' they replied in unison.

They were such good boys, she thought as she slipped out of her black silk coat and hung it in the closet. But they really should have gone to bed as instructed. Although, as John had said, it was probably a good thing they hadn't. Without the teasing interruption they'd provided, there was no telling what she and Bill might have been tempted to do out in the hallway.

Why, she might even have invited him into the apartment for a nightcap.

Just thinking about curling up on the sofa with Bill made Eloise blush as she kicked off her high-heeled black shoes, then reached for the zipper at the back of her dress. They wouldn't have simply sat there for very long if the kiss they had shared in the hallway was any indication. And Eloise had sense enough to know that sharing even a chaste kiss with him wasn't a very good idea under the circumstances.

The issues dividing them hadn't magically faded away over the course of the evening they'd spent together. In fact, those issues would have to be addressed first thing in the morning when she arrived at her Manhattan Multiples office. No amount of wishing otherwise would change that. Nor would any number of shared kisses, whether chaste or intimate.

Though not sworn enemies, she and Bill Harper couldn't really be friends, much less lovers. Not when he had the power to destroy all she had worked so hard to accomplish the past twelve years, she reminded her-

self as she washed her face, brushed her hair, slipped
into her nightgown and then into bed.

And while she understood Bill's reasons for wanting
to cut city funding to nonprofit organizations, she
couldn't, in good conscience, appear to go along with
those reasons by pursuing any kind of personal relationship with him. There were too many good and dedicated
people depending on her and, more important, on Manhattan Multiples for her to be so selfish.

She'd had her downtime—as she had come to think
of that evening—and she had enjoyed it thoroughly. But
she had to face reality in the morning and get busy again
doing whatever she could to save Manhattan Multiples.
Even if that meant staying as far away from Mayor Harper as she could.

And she would, really she would—in the morning.

But now, snuggling under the blankets on her bed,
eyes closed, arms around her linen-covered feather pil-
low, Eloise allowed herself to relive one more time the
soul-stirring kiss she had shared with him so unreserv-
edly, and to consider, as she drifted off to sleep, the
might-have-been that could, and would, never be.

Chapter Three

The muted but monotonous drone of a vacuum cleaner brought Eloise slowly, annoyingly awake. Much to her regret, the remaining wisps of a very pleasant dream faded altogether as she opened her eyes. Beams of sunlight peeked through the slats of the plantation blinds on the bedroom windows, assuring her morning had come.

Only, she didn't really want to get out of bed just yet. She wanted to close her eyes again, snuggle deeper under the blankets and try to recapture the peace and serenity of wherever her sleeping self had been just moments ago. And she tried to do that—for all of the thirty seconds it took her to realize what hearing the sound of the vacuum cleaner meant.

Mrs. Kazinsky, who always arrived at the apartment at nine o'clock sharp on Wednesdays and Fridays, was already busily at work.

Which meant that *she,* in turn, had overslept by at

least three hours from the time when her alarm should have gone off. *Would* have gone off if she hadn't been in such a daze following the Mayor's Ball that she had forgotten to set the darn thing in the first place.

Why hadn't anyone invented an alarm clock that went off at the same time every morning whether you remembered to click the appropriate switch or not? And if someone already had, why hadn't she found one yet?

Grumbling to herself, Eloise tossed aside her blankets and sat up, finally risking a glance at the obstinately ordinary and uncoöperative, though highly decorative, clock on her nightstand.

Ten-fifteen! It couldn't be.

But it was, she chided herself as she hurried toward the master bathroom, then skidded to a halt and headed, instead, for the bedroom door, her disgust at her own lack of discipline—how much effort did it require to set an alarm clock, after all?—having been replaced by concern for her sons.

It was her responsibility to see that Carl, John and Henry got off to school on time every morning—a responsibility she had never taken lightly and had always fulfilled regardless of how late she had been out the night before—well, always in the past.

As she flung open the door and started down the hallway, her agitation mounting, Eloise saw Mrs. Kazinsky backing slowly out of Carl's room, pushing, then pulling the vacuum cleaner as she went. Seeming to sense Eloise's presence in the hallway, the housekeeper looked up, smiled placidly and switched off the vacuum.

"So, Mrs. Vale, you are awake. I am hoping I didn't disturb you, but I had to start on the boys' rooms."

"It's a good thing you did or I might have slept till noon," Eloise reassured her.

She knew Mrs. Kazinsky liked to tackle her sons' rooms first, getting the heaviest cleaning out of the way while she was feeling the most energetic, and she didn't blame the older woman for sticking to her routine. Eloise was the one who had deviated from her usual schedule, one that had her out of the apartment no later than eight-thirty most weekday mornings.

"There's fresh coffee in the pot and I brought some of those pastries from the Polish bakery in my neighborhood that you like," the housekeeper offered, still smiling.

"Sounds wonderful, Mrs. Kazinsky." Eloise smiled gratefully in return, then added, "I take it the boys got off to school okay."

"They were gone when I got here, and there were cereal bowls and glasses in the sink, all rinsed out, too. They are such good boys, Mrs. Vale."

"Yes, they are," Eloise agreed as she headed toward the kitchen, ready for a cup of Mrs. K.'s strong black coffee and one of the buttery rich, cinnamon and nut-filled pastries she had yet to find the willpower to refuse.

She should have known her Carl, John and Henry could, and would, get themselves off to school on their own. They had already convinced her that they were safe at home in the apartment without an adult sitter to supervise them when she attended social engagements in the evening, hadn't they?

They were growing up, she reminded herself, pouring coffee into a china mug, taking a pastry from the bakery box on the counter, then heading back to her bedroom. And they were also growing more and more independent. She was proud of them, of course. She didn't want them tied to her apron strings, clinging to her forever.

That wouldn't have been fair to any of them, herself included.

But at the same time, Eloise felt just a little sad and just a little lost. She had devoted so much of her life to her beloved sons. What would she do once they were truly out on their own, especially if she no longer had Manhattan Multiples to occupy her time? She didn't like the idea of spending her golden years not only all alone, but also without work she enjoyed.

For a fleeting instant, Eloise remembered the kiss she had shared with Bill Harper at her front door the night before, and realized that she didn't necessarily have to be alone. But contemplating a future with Bill was more wishful thinking than anything else.

The physical and emotional attraction between them had been more than obvious. But she couldn't, in good conscience, pursue a relationship with him under the circumstances. His views on city funding for nonprofit organizations made it impossible.

As for having to give up her work at Manhattan Multiples—work she thoroughly enjoyed—*that* she could control, at least to some extent. She hadn't lost the battle to save city funding for her organization yet. And there was still a very good chance that she wouldn't if she got her butt in gear, threw on some clothes and made an effort to get to her office sometime before noon, she reminded herself, making a face at her tousle-haired image in the bathroom mirror.

Worst case scenario, she could, and would if necessary, keep Manhattan Multiples going using her apartment as a base of operations. Granted she would have to scale down considerably, but she would continue to offer as many services as possible. And she would focus on the most important aspect of her work, the one she enjoyed the most—directing a supportive, nurturing network of people as devoted as she was to helping women cope with their multiple birth pregnancies.

She had already brought in quite a bit of money from the fund-raisers she'd been holding for Manhattan Multiples. Of course, that amount wouldn't be nearly enough to cover the costs of maintaining the three floors Manhattan Multiples now occupied in a building on Madison Avenue. It would, however, be enough to pay some salaries, provide counseling services, some classroom instruction and some medical care to those most urgently in need of help.

The scope of her organization would certainly be smaller and the headquarters would have to be relocated, but Manhattan Multiples wouldn't go out of existence altogether. Not if she had anything to do about it, and she had only just begun to tap her personal resources.

Reinvigorated by a hot shower, a second cup of Mrs. Kazinsky's coffee and, yes, another pastry, along with the talk she'd had with herself, Eloise swept a brush through her hair and applied her makeup. Then she dressed quickly in tailored gray wool pants, a black cashmere turtleneck sweater and black, low-heeled leather boots. She completed her outfit with a single strand of pearls and matching pearl-cluster earrings, sophisticated but not showy, snapped the catch of her chunky gold and platinum watch band and was ready to go.

Though the weather report she'd caught on the radio stated that the outdoor temperature was hovering just above freezing, she decided to walk the short distance to her office at Manhattan Multiples. Bundled into her calf-length black cashmere wool coat she would be more than warm enough. And the brisk air and bright sunshine would surely blow away any last cobwebs that might fog her brain.

She had a lot to deal with today, and getting a late start as she already was, she couldn't afford to be anything but at her very best.

The walk did indeed do her good. The sights and sounds of the bustling city and the people moving past her on the sidewalks with seeming strength and purpose, lifted her spirits another notch.

Yes, her beloved New York City had been down for a while following the destructive attacks by a band of mad terrorists. But the city and its people were healing, and signs of renewed faith, hope and love were visible all around her.

Especially within the walls of Manhattan Multiples, Eloise reminded herself with a slight smile as she headed toward the double glass doors that led into the warm and inviting reception area on the first of the organization's three floors.

"Good morning, Ms. Vale," Tony Martino greeted her as he stepped forward and opened one of the doors for her.

A personable young man, five-ten, with a sturdy build, black hair and kind brown eyes, he was the daytime security guard she'd hired after she'd started receiving threatening letters from an anonymous but frighteningly disgruntled man who seemed to despise everything Manhattan Multiples represented. Tony's twin brother, Frank, took over as the nighttime security guard, which was extremely fitting and amused Eloise to no end.

She loved the idea of multiples looking out for the well-being of Manhattan Multiples.

"Good morning, Tony, although I should probably say good afternoon. I'm running way late today."

"Hey, no problem, Ms. Vale. You're the boss. Ain't nobody I know gonna get on your case," Tony replied with an engaging grin. "And if they do, you tell me about it and I'll take care of them for you."

"Thanks, Tony. I will."

The soothing blue of the sky motif covering the wall behind the elegant antique reception desk never failed to lighten Eloise's mood, as did the lovely mix of New Age music piped through the sound system. She recognized a favorite cut from a Danny Wright CD that had been getting lots of play lately.

And with good reason, she acknowledged, seeing Josie Tate Dunnigan, her receptionist, newly wed to Michael Dunnigan and proud mother-to-be huddled with her personal assistant, Allison Baker Perez, also newly wed to Jorge Perez, and expecting. Eloise was more and more certain she would have twins or maybe even triplets if her rapidly expanding tummy was any indication.

Love had been in the air at Manhattan Multiples for several months now, much to Eloise's delight. She had always been a romantic at heart, and having so many of the special women she had come to care about over the past few years finally finding happiness with some very special men had given her great joy. And a great, but very secret, desire to find that same kind of happiness for herself.

Maybe that explained why she had been so attracted to Bill Harper last night. Maybe she had just been overly receptive to *any* possibility of love, and Bill had simply been available. Of course, that would only be the case if her attraction to Bill was something new rather than something she had first felt seventeen years ago and had continued to feel ever since.

Again Eloise remembered the kiss they'd shared, and

again she realized how easily he had swept her off her feet. And would again, she warned herself, given half a chance. Unless she kept in mind the cause she had to support—a cause that was in direct opposition to Mayor Harper's own stated goals for the city.

"Sorry I'm late," Eloise said again to Josie and Allison as she approached the reception desk.

"I would have been surprised if you weren't, all things considered," Allison replied, her smile as teasing as her tone of voice.

Amazing how her formerly oh-so-prim-and-proper personal assistant had changed in the past few months, Eloise thought. Allison could still be businesslike when necessary, but she was so much more relaxed, and so much happier now. Marriage to Jorge Perez and impending motherhood seemed to have made it possible for her to reveal the more lighthearted side of her personality that she had once seemed impelled to hide.

"Nor would I," Josie chorused, still cute as a button and still a free spirit at heart despite her own recent marriage to firefighter Michael Dunnigan and her unexpected, but thoroughly welcome, pregnancy.

Her eyes danced as merrily as Allison's did, making Eloise wonder what kind of news the two of them might have for her. They were in such good humor, not to mention so full of devilry for it to be anything as routine as one of Manhattan Multiples' clients successfully delivering healthy babies.

Though always a cause for celebration, Eloise was sure such an announcement wouldn't have had them quite so…atwitter.

Only as she paused by the reception desk to collect the large sheaf of message slips Josie had ready for her did Eloise spy the source of Josie and Allison's merriment. Spread out on the gleaming cherry wood surface of the reception desk were several of New York City's daily papers. All were open to the Lifestyle section where photographs of the Mayor's Ball were featured prominently.

Not just any photos of the ball, though, Eloise saw at once as she wordlessly picked up one newspaper after another and viewed the pictures more closely. Jumping off the pages were pictures of Bill and her—pictures that showed the two of them having a wonderful time together, as, of course, they had.

But there was so much more revealed in the photographs, and what she saw made Eloise blush hotly all the way to the roots of her smoothly styled ash-blond hair.

"Oh, my..." she murmured, her hands starting to tremble ever so slightly as she studied the look in Bill's eyes as he touched the rim of the champagne glass he held with hers.

The same look was in her eyes as she smiled at him across the small table she had thought hidden away in an alcove. And it was apparent again in both their eyes as they swayed together on the dance floor, their bodies appearing to meld much more closely than she'd realized at the time.

She couldn't believe that two mature adults, as well schooled in the importance of public behavior as she and Bill, had each let down their guards so carelessly and so completely. She didn't know about Bill, but she hadn't intended to wear her heart on her sleeve. Yet it appeared she had done just that, quite blatantly, in fact.

And, Eloise admitted, quite honestly, as well.

Here, for her and the whole world to see was proof that she was still in love with Bill Harper. And if the expression on his face was any indication, not only was the feeling most definitely mutual, but also a source of great delight for the newspapers' headline writers.

"The Mayor and Manhattan Multiples Maven—Enemies No More?" read one. And "Ms. Vale v. the Mayor—All Bets Off!!!" read another of the more sensational banners under the photographs. Eloise was almost afraid to read the accompanying text, although she knew she must.

"You look lovely in the pictures," Allison said, as if sensing her need for reassurance. "And the articles I've read are pretty fairly divided as to which one of you has possibly gone over to the other side."

"Well, that's something for which to be grateful," Eloise replied. She quickly scanned first one article that claimed she now went along with the mayor's cuts in funding, then another saying the mayor must certainly have been charmed into rethinking *his* long-held position. "Everyone could have assumed I'd given in completely. Especially considering the sappy look it obviously appears I had on my face all evening."

"You don't look sappy at all," Josie retorted. "You look like a woman in love, and Mayor Harper appears to be positively smitten, as well. How could that not work in our favor?"

"Mayor Harper isn't the type to allow personal relationships to get in the way of public policy," Eloise pointed out pragmatically.

In fact, he wasn't the type to allow a personal relationship to get in the way of any action he deemed necessary for the public good. She had learned that the hard way seventeen years ago when his very earliest political aspirations and involvement had been of primary importance to him. But such an in-depth explanation would only serve to stir up Josie and Allison's curiosity that much more.

"Maybe he just hasn't met his match till now," Allison suggested with a knowing smile.

Her life had turned around completely since Jorge Perez had entered her life, and so had Jorge's. The same was true of Josie and Michael. Thus Eloise chose to forgive them both for fantasizing a similar happy ending for her. She also resisted the urge to offer elaborate explanations as to why such an outcome would never be possible for her and Bill.

"I may be his match, but that gleam he seems to have in his eyes is hardly the result of affection for me," she stated in a dismissive tone. "He's simply enjoying our latest and first face-to-face confrontation."

Since she and Bill hadn't actually discussed their differing viewpoints last night, Eloise knew she was stretching the truth. But if she succeeded in throwing Allison and Josie off track, maybe the rumors of a budding romance between her and the mayor apparently already stirring in the press would be quickly put to rest.

"So you don't feel as if you made any headway in convincing Mayor Harper to reconsider his proposed cuts to city funding?" Allison asked, her ever-present concern over the possible closing of Manhattan Multiples echoing in her voice.

"I can't honestly say that I did," Eloise replied, her cheeks burning all over again.

She could only imagine what Allison and Josie would think if they knew she had been so enamored of the mayor that she hadn't brought up the issues dividing them even one time while she had been with him last night. The two young women were depending on Manhattan Multiples for their livelihoods as well as for much-needed support during their pregnancies. So were a lot of other women.

Eloise had admitted that she'd been a selfish socialite partying hearty last night, and downtime or not, she was more than a little ashamed of herself just then.

"At least a lot of people seem to think you did," Josie pointed out, waving a hand at the newspapers. "As Allison said, the articles are pretty fairly divided. Some of the reporters seem to think progress has been made in favor of our side of the issue, and some in favor of the mayor's side. It's more than obvious that you're a force to be reckoned with. Otherwise your presence at the ball with Mayor Harper wouldn't have rated such publicity."

"And I'd better take full advantage of it before Mayor Harper makes a final decision." Tossing the newspapers aside, Eloise picked up the pink slips of paper containing her telephone messages and turned toward the hallway that led to her office. "Allison, make an appointment for me to meet with Mayor Harper later today. A follow-up to our outing last night seems to be in order."

"I'll get right on it," Allison replied, gathering the newspapers into her arms, then following Eloise down the hallway.

Having gotten such a late start to the day, Eloise concentrated first on returning as many telephone calls as she could. Some were from acquaintances wanting to chat about the personal aspects of her date with the mayor. Those people she politely cut short. Others were from supporters of Manhattan Multiples congratulating her on having gotten the mayor's attention at last. Those people she thanked graciously while also requesting that they continue to fight to save city funding for nonprofit organizations, reminding them the battle hadn't actually been won yet.

Early in the afternoon, Eloise also had a visit from Leah Simpson, the pregnant homeless woman she and the staff of Manhattan Multiples had made a special effort to help over the past few months. Leah now had a small but tidy apartment of her own. She was also currently on paid maternity leave from her job as a clerk at Manhattan Multiples, and had been keeping busy caring for her newborn triplet daughters, fondly and appreciatively named Eloise, Allison and Josie.

All three babies, dressed in darling little outfits and secured safely in the triple-seat stroller Eloise had given Leah at the baby shower they'd held for her at the office, were glowing with good health. Leah, too, seemed to be doing well, though she was understandably tired.

With the help of various friends she'd made at Manhattan Multiples, however, she seemed to be coping with the stress of caring for three tiny babies. And finally more confident of her own ability to take care of herself and her babies, she no longer seemed inclined to reconcile with the alcoholic and abusive husband who had left her when she was pregnant.

The only negative aspect of Eloise's day came in the form of yet another in a series of increasingly angry anonymous letters that arrived with the afternoon mail. So far, nothing overt had happened at Manhattan Multiples as a result of the threatening letters. But they had been of enough concern to Eloise that she was grateful to have security guards.

Today's letter included accusations that her organization in general and Eloise in particular had conspired to break up a man's family. So the threats were coming from the husband of one of their clients, she thought, having not been completely sure until then of the letter writer's connection to Manhattan Multiples.

But who was he, and more important, who among Manhattan Multiples' many clients was related to him? She would be the one most in danger if the man became enraged enough to do physical harm because she would be the one normally most close at hand.

Eloise would have to ask the various staff members if they knew of anyone on Manhattan Multiples' list of clients who might possibly be currently involved in a problematic relationship or had talked about difficulties of any kind in her marriage. She would also have to seriously consider contacting the police.

She didn't want to panic either the staff or their clients, but neither did she want to endanger anyone by failing to take proper protective measures. The Martino brothers provided a certain degree of security. But even they could be hurt if the letter writer was as crazy as he had now begun to sound, and suddenly turned violent.

By the time Eloise had sorted through the rest of her mail, nibbling on a tuna sandwich as she scribbled responses for Allison to type, it was after three o'clock. Surprised at how fast the time had flown by, she sat back in her chair, ready to relax.

Then she remembered her request of Allison earlier to set up an appointment for her to meet with the mayor. She reached out to buzz her on the intercom, but before she could, Allison bustled into the office as quickly as her burgeoning belly would allow, a frown on her normally sunny face.

"I know, I know. I was supposed to make an appointment for you to meet with Mayor Harper," she said, sitting wearily in one of the two wing chairs facing Eloise's desk.

"No luck?"

"I've been trying for hours just to get through to his

chief of staff. The receptionist kept putting me on hold, then conveniently disconnecting my call. When Wally Phillips finally deigned to speak to me, he told me the mayor was all booked up, not only today, but also every day for the next two weeks. He said there was no way Mayor Harper could spare you even five minutes of his precious time. I'm sorry, Eloise, but I'm not sure what else I can do to get you a slot on the mayor's busy schedule.''

"Nothing that I can think of, either," Eloise replied. "Thanks for trying, though." She pushed away from her desk resolutely. "Now it's time for me to take matters into my own hands."

"How do you intend to do that?" Allison looked up at her warily.

"I'm going over to Mayor Harper's office right now, appointment or not, and I'm going to make my presence there known to all the reporters and photographers who hang around City Hall. Mayor Harper will have to see me then or he'll end up losing all the benefit he got from those pictures in the papers this morning. I don't think 'Jilted Socialite Angrily Demands Audience with Mayor' would play well with his constituents, do you?''

"No, it most certainly wouldn't," Allison answered with a delighted laugh. "Shall I call the limousine service for you?"

"Why, yes, that sounds like a good idea," Eloise agreed. "I could probably get there faster on foot at this time of day, but my arrival wouldn't be nearly as attention getting, would it?"

"Not nearly." Allison laughed again as she pushed out of the chair.

"Twins," Eloise said.

"What?"

Allison paused in the doorway of Eloise's office and eyed her with surprise.

"Twins, at least. Maybe triplets. You're getting awfully big awfully fast, sweetie."

"Oh, please, don't say that," Allison pleaded, a hint of fear in her lovely eyes. "I can't imagine how I'm going to handle one baby, much less multiples."

"You'll have lots of help, of course. That's why I started Manhattan Multiples in the first place, and that's why I have every intention of keeping our organization going—to help you and lots of other pregnant women. But first I have to have a little talk with the mayor."

"I'll call the limousine service."

"Have you thought about scheduling a sonogram with Dr. Cross?" Eloise continued, still eyeing her assistant with consideration.

"Oh, it's way too soon."

"Not if you're having multiples."

Allison, looking just a little green around the gills, rolled her eyes and hurried out of Eloise's office, leaving Eloise the one now laughing with delight.

Chapter Four

"Yes, James, I understand how important it is to stand firm on my proposed cuts to city funding for nonprofit organizations. I wouldn't have initiated them in the first place if I hadn't thought they were necessary for the good of the city as a whole."

Sitting back in his desk chair, Mayor Bill Harper barely contained a sigh of exasperation as he reassured yet another supporter that he hadn't gone soft on special interests. James Hargrove, CEO of Power Industries, Inc.—a major company that would benefit greatly if New York City could be pulled out of its recession—seemed somewhat mollified.

"Well, you can't blame me for being concerned, Mr. Mayor," James replied formally, foregoing his usual Bill-old-buddy form of address to emphasize the seriousness with which he viewed their conversation. "You seemed to be getting mighty cozy with that Vale woman at the ball last night. I'm sure I'm not the only one who's been wondering if she managed to win you over to her side of the fence. She's one forceful little woman, from what I've seen, and she certainly hasn't been shy about making her feelings known where your proposed cuts are concerned.''

''I don't blame you at all, James. I admit I found Ms. Vale's company most enjoyable at the ball. And yes, Ms. Vale can be a very charming and persuasive woman. But let me assure you again that my position on city funding hasn't changed because we attended the ball together. Surely you know me well enough by now to trust my judgment.''

''Yes, of course, Mr. Mayor.''

''I appreciate your concern, James. But there's absolutely no need for you to worry.''

''It's important that we get this city back on its feet again, not just for a business like mine, but for the population as a whole,'' Hargrove blustered, obviously eager not to appear totally self-serving.

''And that's my main goal right now,'' Bill assured him one last time. ''Take care, James, and please keep in touch.''

''Will do, Mr. Mayor.''

Reaching out, Bill cradled the telephone receiver. Then he sat back again and finally allowed himself to utter the sigh he'd been holding inside himself for the better part of the day. Caused by annoyance more than anything, it nonetheless held more than a hint of weariness, as well.

He had arrived at his office in City Hall just after six o'clock that morning—long before he'd expected any of his staff members to show up since they, too, had attended the ball last night. Though he didn't make a habit of it, he could get by on five or six hours of sleep when necessary—a good thing today because he'd barely managed that amount last night.

His mind had been too full of thoughts of Eloise Vale for him to do much more than toss and turn in bed until he'd finally given up on sleep altogether shortly before dawn.

The time he had spent with her—from the moment she had opened her apartment door to him until the moment he had ended, reluctantly, the kiss they'd shared, much to her sons' amusement—had been truly wonderful.

He had prepared himself for a cool and distant, oh-so-proper and polite reception from her. That she had been warm and welcoming, open and obviously at ease with him had surprised him only momentarily.

Eloise could have chosen to forget the good times they had once shared, but instead she had seemed to remember the past as fondly as he, and to be as eager as he to renew their former camaraderie.

She hadn't pressured him once regarding the divisive issues about which they'd battled at a distance the past few months as he'd fully expected she would. In fact, she hadn't brought those issues—so important to both of them—into their conversation in any but the most casual of ways all evening. And, more than content just to enjoy her company, neither had he.

What had initially been intended as a placating measure—an effort to reason with Eloise in order to end her more vociferous attacks against his cost-cutting proposals in the media—had become a very personal campaign to win back the woman he had never stopped loving. And surely, if the kiss she had allowed him to steal was any indication, he had made at least a tiny inroad in that direction.

Bill had thought long and hard about kissing her during the ride back to her apartment in the limousine. He hadn't been sure about the wisdom of initiating such an intimacy under the circumstances. He had considered it questionable, at best.

But then she had turned all cool and distant and polite on him, extending her hand, thanking him in an almost haughty tone as they'd stood by her front door. He hadn't been able to resist the sudden urge to remind her of what they had once shared and now had a chance to share again. If only they could get past their basic disagreement about the need to cut city funding.

And Eloise had liked the reminder. She had liked it very, very much, indeed.

As he'd lain in the deep night darkness, alone in his bed, trying desperately to fall asleep, Bill had recalled just how ardently she'd returned his kiss before her sons interrupted them. And he'd had no doubt that she had not only enjoyed their kiss just as much as he, but had also been as sorry as he that they couldn't take it any further.

Thoughts of where they might have gone from that first luscious kiss had been the last straw for him. Suddenly too restless to stay in bed a moment longer, Bill had dressed quickly. Then he had made his own way to city hall, enjoying a rare taste of anonymity as he walked along the still mostly deserted city sidewalks.

His first inkling of what the day held in store for him came when he sat at his desk, savoring the relative silence surrounding him along with a cup of the coffee he had brewed himself in the community pot. It was then that he began to read the first of the newspapers delivered to his office each morning.

In all honesty, the articles written about the Mayor's Ball and his presence there with Eloise hadn't been any worse than he'd expected. He was a public figure and so, to a certain extent, was she. What they did and didn't do made for interesting copy.

Depending on the viewpoint of the reporter, the copy that day declared that either Eloise or he was about to go over to the other side. And luckily, the viewpoints were evenly enough divided not to be a major cause for concern.

The photographs of him with Eloise, on the other hand, were so revealing that Bill had felt the long-forgotten heat of a blush warm his face as he studied them one after another. In every picture he seemed to be wearing his heart on his sleeve for all to see, as all would who looked through the daily papers.

He had thought he'd mastered the art of hiding his true feelings years ago, at least in a public setting. But that obviously hadn't been the case last night. He had enjoyed Eloise's company so much that he hadn't even thought to pretend otherwise.

Even though it would have been politically savvy to do so, as he'd been reminded by various members of his staff when they'd filtered into the office after him—especially Wally Phillips, his main assistant—and as he'd also been reminded when he'd fielded one phone call after another once the switchboard had opened that morning.

The intercom buzzed, jolting Bill, much too soon for his liking, from the few minutes respite he'd had. A glance at the crystal clock on his desk told him it was after four. He'd already put in a ten-hour day. He wasn't sure he had the patience to deal with another demanding constituent.

In fact, he wasn't sure, at that moment, that he had enough patience left to deal with another demanding constituent the remainder of the month, maybe even the remainder of the year.

What he really, really, *really* wanted to do was whisk Eloise away to his secluded house in the Hamptons—the one place he had always considered his home—and pick up where they'd been forced to leave off the night before. Only he was, by choice, the mayor of New York City, and she was not only a businesswoman, but also the mother of three teenage sons with responsibilities of her own.

Again the intercom buzzed, annoying him more than it should.

"What?" he demanded, making no effort at all to hide the testiness in his tone.

"Sorry to bother you again, sir," Wally Phillips, his assistant, began, not actually sounding apologetic but, rather, exasperated in his own way.

Wally hadn't had an especially good day himself, running interference as he'd done since early that morning, Bill conceded.

"That's all right, Wally. What is it now?" he asked in a milder tone.

"I have Frances Wegner, the president of Construction Services, on line one. He wants to talk to you about the city funding cuts—big surprise. Also, Charles Goodwin, a reporter with the *Daily Express,* wants to set up an interview with you. I can pencil him in for next Monday afternoon. I recommend you talk to him. He's an up-and-comer and he's been fair-minded on past issues."

"I'll talk to Goodwin Monday afternoon. Tell Wegner I've stepped out of the office. I'll call him tomorrow."

"Are you sure—"

"I'm sure, Wally. I'll talk to Wegner first thing tomorrow morning."

"All right, sir…"

When Wally didn't click off the intercom immediately, Bill bit back a sigh and asked with as much equanimity as he could muster, "Is there something else you wanted to tell me?"

"Well, actually, Ms. Vale is here," Wally replied, his hesitation evident.

"Here?" Bill repeated, his heart beating a little faster as he sat straighter in his desk chair.

"Yeah—right here, right now. Her assistant called earlier this afternoon to make an appointment for her to see you today. I told her we couldn't schedule her for at least two weeks. That's not exactly true, but we already know how she feels about your proposed cuts to city funding. Also, you were together just last night."

"Indeed, we were," Bill muttered.

"Next thing I know, Ms. Vale shows up here demanding to see you. She's obviously not very happy, and she's making no effort to hide it. The City Hall stringers for all the local papers are eating it up, taking pictures, talking to her. I'm thinking you'd better see her. Maybe you could try to calm her down a little, then make an appearance with her while the photographers are still here—happy faces on again like last night."

The very last thing Bill wanted just then was another confrontation, especially with Eloise. He'd had to battle accusations all day that he was going soft on special interests. Now he was going to have to sit by quietly while she accused him of being a heartless hard-liner—

something he couldn't, and most definitely wouldn't, deny when it came to pulling the city out of its recession.

He knew how important Manhattan Multiples was to her. But it was equally important to him to strengthen the morale of the entire city.

Had she come to see him for any other reason, she wouldn't be in such a snit. And had she come to see him for any other reason, he would have welcomed her into his office with open arms.

"Sir? Are you there?" Wally ventured.

"Of course I'm here, although I'd rather be just about anywhere else right now," Bill retorted, then drew a calming breath.

It wasn't fair to Wally to take out his irritation on him. He was only doing his job, and doing it quite well, all things considered.

"That makes two of us, Mr. Mayor," Wally admitted. "However…"

"Yes, however…we're here and so is Ms. Vale. Please show her into my office and I'll see what I can do to make her happy."

Bill doubted there was anything he could accomplish in that direction even before his assistant graciously escorted Eloise into his office. One look at her, striding purposefully along behind Wally, her pale-gray eyes shooting daggers and her luscious mouth grimly set, and he was convinced that it was futile to even try.

"Eloise, how good to see you again." Standing to greet her, Bill extended his hand across the cluttered surface of his desk and offered his most charming smile as he added, "I was going to call you later."

She gazed at him long and hard, her eyes narrowing dangerously, appearing to be not the least bit mollified by his cordial manner. Then, ignoring his outstretched hand, she shrugged out of her long black coat, tossed it onto one of the matching leather chairs positioned in front of his desk, and sat gracefully in the other.

She was almost as lovely when she was angry as she was when she was ecstatically happy, Bill noted as she primly folded her hands in her lap. But he knew better than to say as much to her when her mind seemed so obviously occupied by the business they had between them.

At least, he didn't *think* she was there to discuss personal issues. In fact, considering her current mood, he hoped, more than anything that *wasn't* why she'd barged into his office so unceremoniously.

"Obviously you've seen today's papers," she began at last, her tone revealing only the slightest hint of anger as she waved a hand at the newsprint spread out on his desk.

"Yes, I have. Lots of pictures of us. We certainly looked like we were having a good time together," he ventured, modulating his own tone carefully while softening his smile to one of encouragement. "I, for one, enjoyed myself more than I have in a very long time. Being with you was really wonderful, Eloise."

Bill knew he was skating on very thin ice with her. But he couldn't resist reminding her that they *had* had fun together last night. And that the attraction between them *had* sparked with the same hot current of electric desire as it had seventeen years ago.

Eloise's determination to maintain a combative stance seemed to waiver just a bit. Her pale eyes widened at his words, and the grim line drawing her mouth tight softened noticeably. But then, a moment later she gathered herself again and continued in a pragmatic manner that gave no quarter.

"I enjoyed being with you, too, Mr. Mayor. What I haven't enjoyed, however, is dealing with the fallout that's resulted. All day today I've had to field one call after another from the people who have fought along with me all these months to maintain city funding for our nonprofit organizations. Those pictures in the papers have had them believing I've gone over to *your* side, and we both know that isn't true."

"I've had similar calls myself accusing me of softening up on the issue of cuts in city funding, and we both know *that* isn't true, either. We're on opposite sides of a very important issue, but that doesn't mean we can't have a friendly personal relationship. Look at Mary Matlin and James Carville," he suggested with a flash of brilliance that amazed him. "She's a Republican and he's a Democrat. They never agree on anything politically, but they're actually quite happily married."

"But that's just it, Bill. I *don't* disagree with you politically. At least I haven't until now. I've voted for you every time you've run for office in the state of New York," Eloise shot back heatedly. "And we don't have to be on opposite sides of the city funding issue, either. You know how much nonprofit organizations like Manhattan Multiples have contributed to the welfare of people around the city. We provide jobs and services that wouldn't be available if we didn't exist. But we're not going to be able to continue to exist without the city funds we've always been able to depend upon in the past."

"I realize that, Eloise. Really, I do. Don't think I haven't already taken into account all you've said because I have. Yes, nonprofit organizations contribute to the well-being of the people of New York City, but on a very specialized and selective basis. My goal in redirecting funds once set aside for such organizations is to pull the entire city out of its recession and provide a better standard of living for *all* of the city's residents as a direct result.''

"Even if by doing that you'll also be destroying everything I've worked to create over the past twelve years?'' Eloise demanded, her eyes flashing angrily again.

"I'm not out to destroy anything—certainly not anything you, of all people, value,'' Bill retorted, now feeling more than a little angry himself at her wrongful assumptions. "I'm not that much of an ogre. Hell, I'm not an ogre at all, and I shouldn't have to defend myself as if I am, especially to you.

"But as mayor of this city I have to make choices on how funds are spent, and I have to make those choices based on who will benefit most in the long run. I'm more concerned about all those people out there who don't have any alternatives right now. The way I see it, a non-profit organization taking up three floors in a high-rent building on Madison Avenue has some alternatives when it comes to cutting costs to accommodate the lack of city funding.''

He knew he had gone too far the moment the words left his mouth even if he believed what he'd said—as he did. The look on Eloise's face was first one of shock, then outrage that she made no attempt at all to disguise.

"Are you suggesting that I'm out of touch with *real* people who have what you consider *real* problems because Manhattan Multiples happens to be located on Madison Avenue?'' Rising from her chair, Eloise took a step toward him, then stopped when she came up against the edge of his desk. Leaning forward, she shook a finger at him as her voice escalated. "Well, let me tell you something, Bill Harper. I know just as much about real people with real problems as you do, maybe even more because I've actually worked with them at a hands-on level while you sit here in your elegantly appointed office, dictating—''

He couldn't help himself. At least that's what he told himself in the instant before he stood up, reached out and grabbed Eloise's bossy finger. Just couldn't help himself, especially since there seemed to be no other way to end her self-righteous tirade other than to lean forward and kiss her suddenly momentarily silent, but still slightly open, mouth.

No sense mincing around with one of those half-hearted little pecks, either. Might as well put his soul into it and truly earn the shove-off he fully expected her to give him.

She did stiffen up at the first touch of his lips to hers and she did put her free hand on his shoulder, but she didn't push him away. When he teased her mouth with the tip of his tongue, she drew in a sharp breath, then she relaxed noticeably and teased back with hers. Her hand on his shoulder tightened as if she needed to hold on to him, spurring him on even more.

He threaded the fingers of his free hand through her hair, angling her head to maximize his access, and deepened their kiss another degree. Again Eloise followed his lead, teasing back with her tongue, seeming as hungry as he for the intimate contact they shared.

Bill wasn't really surprised. Eloise had always been a passionate woman—passionate about the causes she chose to champion and passionate about the people for whom she cared. And she had never been one to hide her feelings. She was much too honest to dissemble even when it could work to her advantage.

She was also the last person on earth with whom he wanted to be at odds. Especially when he knew that if he followed his conscience he would be forced to make choices that would ultimately cause her pain.

The buzzing of the intercom, loud and grating to Bill's ears, interrupted them with aggravating efficiency. Though surprised by the sound of it, Bill wasn't as startled as Eloise.

She pulled away from him immediately, ending all physical contact between them. Tucking her hands in the side pockets of her wool pants, she took a decisive step back from where she'd been standing near the edge of his desk, the look on her lovely face one of utter dismay.

Bill wanted to move around his desk, gather her into his arms and assure her that everything would be all right because he would find a way to make it so. Instead, he tucked his hands in his own pockets, as well, and growled an answer to his assistant's untimely summons.

"What now, Wally?"

"Sorry to bother you, Mayor, but it's after five o'clock. You're supposed to be at the convention center by six to say a few words before the basketball game between the New York City firefighters and police officers. The limousine will be out front in five minutes."

"Thanks for the reminder, Wally. I'd forgotten about it completely."

"That's what I'm here for, sir."

While Bill had been speaking to his assistant, Eloise had retrieved her coat and purse from the chair beside her. Now holding both clutched to her chest, she gazed fixedly at a spot somewhere over his left shoulder.

"I...appreciate your time, Mr. Mayor. Thank you for letting me present my case," she said, scrupulously polite as she enunciated each syllable. "I hope you'll give some thought to reconsidering your proposed cuts to—"

"Hey, Eloise...want to go to a basketball game?" he asked. "I can promise we'll have the best seats in the house. I'll even treat you to a hot dog and a beer."

He hated it when she turned formal on him and insisted on acting businesslike. Even more, he hated the thought of having to let her go so soon and in such a mood.

For the second time in two days they'd shared a kiss that promised to take them places he, for one, definitely wanted to go, only to be rudely interrupted. And he was afraid he wasn't going to get many more chances to pursue all the intriguing possibilities that came to his mind unless he found a way for them to be together.

"Oh, really, I couldn't," she began, her pale eyes wary as she reluctantly met his gaze. "The boys—"

"They're more than welcome to join us, too." Bill cut in, his tone jaunty. "We can swing by your apartment and pick them up. They like basketball, don't they?"

"Yes, they do, and they really wanted to go to this particular game," Eloise admitted. "They listened to one of the local radio stations almost nonstop for a week trying to win tickets since all the seats were sold out almost immediately."

"Well then, it's their lucky night, and mine if you'll accept my invitation," Bill said, finally moving around his desk to stand before her. Reaching out, he touched a hand to her cheek and brushed back a wisp of her ash-blond hair. "Come on, Eloise, we'll have fun. And..." he added with a wolfish grin, "you'll get even more positive publicity for your organization by being seen with me yet again."

"Just what I need—another day of reassuring supporters."

"I'm game if you are, sweetheart. And think of how high your stock will rise with your sons."

"There is that," she conceded. "They'd never forgive me for refusing your invitation."

"Then I recommend you don't."

"All right, we'll go to the game with you."

"That's my girl."

Exuberantly Bill pulled Eloise into his arms and hugged her close, coat, purse and all. He was about to steal another quick kiss when the intercom buzzed yet again.

"Coming, Wally," he muttered as he let go of Eloise and went to collect his suit jacket and overcoat from the rack in the corner of his office.

"I'll call the boys and tell them we're on our way," Eloise said, fishing her cell phone from her purse. "They can meet us out in front of our building to save some time."

"Good idea," Bill agreed, smiling at her as he shrugged into his coat.

The excited smile she sent his way in return made his heart sing. And when she took his arm naturally and unselfconsciously as they left his office, his soul glowed with sudden warmth.

He had often felt lonely at public appearances, even in the midst of a crowd of personal supporters. But not tonight, he thought. Tonight he would have Eloise and her sons with him. And for a short time at least, he could pretend they really were together in all the ways that mattered most to him.

Chapter Five

"Together we can continue to rebuild our great city, but only if some changes are made in the way city funds are spent. The good of the entire population of New York City must come before that of special interest groups, no matter how worthy their causes."

Pausing to add emphasis to his words, Bill looked out over the capacity crowd filling the convention center auditorium. Along with everyone else in the audience, Eloise sat quietly, drawn into rapt attention by the mayor's modulated tones.

He was an extremely polished public speaker. He addressed the people without written notes, his stance at the podium relaxed despite the bank of microphones he faced. And while his delivery wasn't exactly folksy, he exuded an air of genuine warmth and caring. He said what he believed to be true, and he said it in such a way that even *she* was tempted to side with him.

As if he'd been reading her mind, Bill directed his gaze her way, his slight smile full of encouragement. *Trust me,* he seemed to be saying across the wide expanse of the basketball court that separated them. *Trust me and everything will be all right.*

How she wished she could do just that, Eloise thought. But if she gambled on his good intentions and lost, the price would be enormously high. And she wouldn't be the only one forced to pay for her mistake. A lot of innocent people would have to pay, as well.

"Hey, Mom, I think he likes you," Carl whispered in a teasing tone as he nudged her gently with his elbow.

Beside him in the courtside row where they had all been seated, John and Henry grinned at her mischievously, as well.

Feeling a blush heat her face, Eloise directed a warning look at her sons, brooking no nonsense, then turned her attention back to Bill as he continued with his speech.

"It is not, however, my intention to force the nonprofit organizations that have, in the past, contributed so much to our city to close their doors altogether. The work they do is necessary and important. But I believe that with donations from private corporations and some restructuring of current budgets, those organizations can, and will, continue to provide much-needed services to our citizens. If we all work together for the common good, we will all come out winners.

"The same is true of the two teams here tonight. By participating in this very special event, every team member, whether firefighter or police office, is a winner. You men and women represent the heart and soul of our city. One team will inevitably walk away with the trophy. That's the nature of the game. But we will all be much better off because of the spirit of camaraderie you display here tonight.

"Let's all follow the example of our firefighters and police officers. Let's all work together for the good of each other and our wonderful city."

All around Eloise, the thunder of enthusiastic applause sounded as Bill stepped back from the podium. Signaling the end of his speech with a wave to the audience, now standing as one body to show their support and approval of their city's elected leader, he then headed across the court to take the empty chair beside her.

Standing, too, Eloise applauded along with her sons, who were inspired enough to also add a few shrill whistles and a "right on" or two.

In his speech Bill had used the same argument to support his proposed cuts in funding as he had during their much more private meeting in his office earlier. Then, Eloise had lashed back at him furiously, taking major exception to what she'd heard as an accusation of snobbery on her part.

Now, in a calmer frame of mind and not quite so much on the defensive, she could admit, albeit grudgingly, that some of his points were well taken.

Private corporations and wealthy individuals had already increased their generous financial contributions to Manhattan Multiples through the fund-raisers she had organized. And she had already determined that Manhattan Multiples didn't have to take up three floors of a high-rent Madison Avenue building to continue to provide its very special services to those in need.

Still, there was a certain amount of principle involved in her angry debate with the mayor. Manhattan Multiples had thrived with the help of city funding. Without that money there was a chance it would become so much less than it was now, not to mention so much less than she had always intended it to be in the future.

As Bill stood beside her and acknowledged the still-applauding crowd with a big grin and another wave of his hand, Eloise looked up at him. He was so handsome and so charming and so darned sexy. He could get just about anyone to believe just about anything he wanted, including, on occasion, her. Knowing that, she had to constantly remind herself to beware. But sometimes it was hard to heed the warning bells ringing in her head.

Times like now, she thought as he turned his gaze on her, his smile softening into something a little more special, a little more secret. And times like that afternoon when he'd grabbed her wagging finger and silenced her angry tirade with a deep and all too delicious kiss.

The memory alone of how quickly and easily she had succumbed to him made her blush all over again.

"Can we call a truce?" he had asked as he'd led her out of his office and into the elevator that took them down to the waiting limousine.

"Just for tonight," she'd replied primly, trying to regain some of her lost composure, her attempt causing him to chuckle.

"So tell me, Ms. Vale, who do you think will win the game?" he'd asked as they drove the short distance to her apartment to pick up her sons.

"The firefighters, for sure," she answered without hesitation.

"And why is that?"

"No doughnuts to weigh them down," she'd stated merrily.

"Poor police officers always getting a bad rap where their eating habits are concerned."

"The security guards at Manhattan Multiples are police officers, too, and they're always bringing us dough-nuts.''

"You have security guards at Manhattan Multiples?'' Bill had eyed her with sudden concern. "Have you been having problems there?''

"I hired them more as a precaution than anything else,'' she'd hedged, not wanting to have to tell Bill about the threatening letters she'd been receiving when she wasn't really worried about them herself. Seeing her sons dancing around excitedly on the sidewalk outside her apartment building, she had quickly changed the subject. "Looks like they're ready to have some fun.''

"Then that makes at least four of us,'' Bill had said, his voice lightening again, though his eyes had still held a faint shadow of anxiety.

"Five of us,'' Eloise had stated, reaching out to give his arm a reassuring squeeze.

"Five of us, then.'' Bill had smiled at her with obvious delight, then he'd opened the door of the limousine and greeted her sons with a "Hey, guys, pile in,'' which they'd done amidst much laughing and pushing as they'd jockeyed for the best seats.

"Great speech, Mr. Mayor,'' Carl said now, drawing Bill's attention back to the present moment. The boy reached around Eloise to offer his hand in a gentlemanly salute.

"Yeah, great speech, sir,'' John and Henry echoed, leaving their seats so they could also shake his hand.

"Thanks, Carl, and you, too, John and Henry,'' he replied, miraculously naming each triplet correctly as he graciously accepted their praise.

"I can't believe you did that,'' Eloise murmured, un-able to hide the wonder in her voice.

"What? My speech?" Bill asked, eyeing her warily as they finally took their seats.

"No, not that. You got all their names right."

"Their shirts are the same, but each one of them is wearing a different color," he explained, obviously proud, and rightly so, of his powers of observation. "Now, about my speech…what did you think?"

"It was a great speech, very…thought provoking," Eloise admitted, her gaze sliding away from his as she reminded herself, yet again, that they were still on opposite sides of a very serious issue.

"That's good," he said, sliding an arm around her shoulders companionably. "I like to provoke as many thoughts as possible whenever possible."

"Why am I not surprised?" She quirked a look at him again, one eyebrow raised.

"Because you know me too well."

"Not really," she replied, aware that after seventeen years apart he was actually a stranger to her in many important ways.

"Then we'll have to do something about that, won't we?"

Eloise wasn't sure what to say in response. On a personal level, she wanted to know Bill Harper…intimately. But on a professional level she'd be so much better off keeping *Mayor* Harper at a very discreet distance.

In any case, whatever answer she might have chosen to give, the renewed cheering of the crowd would have drowned it out. To the blare of a brass band, the two teams, one made up of New York City firefighters, the other made up of New York City police officers took to the basketball court from opposite sides of the auditorium.

Both teams had warmed up before Bill's speech. Likewise, the national anthem had also been sung, so the game could begin without too much further ado. There was the requisite flexing of muscles, leering and sneering from the friendly rivals, then the tip-off and play was underway.

Distracted by the action on the court, Eloise was quickly drawn into the game. Though she favored the firefighters to win, she cheered easily and equally for each side, as did Bill and her sons, especially when one team member or another got off an exceptional shot.

Sitting so close to the players made the game even more exciting for her. And being there in the company of her sons and Bill gave her a special sense of belonging she hadn't experienced since Walter's death.

As he had at the Mayor's Ball, Bill made sure she, as well as the boys, had whatever they wanted to eat and drink. Surprisingly hungry, she ate two hot dogs smothered in spicy mustard and her favorite sweet pickle relish. She even drank a beer, icy cold and foamy, just the way she liked it.

During the intermissions, Bill had mayoral duties to perform—meeting and greeting as many constituents as he could. He made a point of including her, introducing her to everyone, then standing back while she, too, shook hands and exchanged comments with the various New York City movers and shakers in attendance.

Though rowdy during the game play, Carl, John and Henry were on their best behavior during the intermissions, smiling and shaking hands and making her extremely proud. Of course, she also caught them preening for the press photographers, but at least they weren't making monkey faces.

Their pictures would be in the papers tomorrow along with photos of her and Bill. She couldn't say she was happy about it, but it was unavoidable under the circumstances. It was also a small price to pay for all the fun they were having together at the game.

The firefighters won just as Eloise had predicted. However, the game was so close that the police officers had no reason to be anything but proud of themselves, as well. To more thunderous applause, Bill presented the fire chief with the trophy that would travel from fire station to fire station throughout the city where it would be displayed in the year ahead.

Then, as the stands began to empty and people began to head home, Bill and she along with her sons were escorted out to the limousine and whisked away from the convention center in what seemed like record time.

"Anybody feel like stopping for ice cream?" Bill asked as he relaxed into his seat and took Eloise's hand in his.

The boys immediately chorused their positive reception to his suggestion. Eloise, too, found she had a taste for something sweet to top off the evening, and didn't protest.

Bill directed the chauffeur to a café in the Little Italy neighborhood where the desserts were a destination all on their own. Because it was later on a weeknight, they were able to get a table without waiting. There was a murmur of recognition among the other diners as they were seated, but then they were left to themselves.

The boys ordered huge ice cream concoctions, Bill had a slice of Italian cream cake and coffee, and Eloise decided on a dish of spumoni and a cappuccino. They replayed the game as they ate, recalling great shots, near misses and total flubs with exuberant detail. And they all agreed it was one of the best basketball games they'd seen in a long time because it had been so spirited and the scoring so close.

Finally, their dishes empty, the boys began to yawn.

"Time for me to get you guys home," Bill said, collecting his credit card from the tray left by their waiter.

"Yes, you'd better," Eloise agreed. "They have school tomorrow, and this is the second night in a row they've been up past their normal bedtime."

"Aw, Mom, it's not that late. It's not even midnight yet," Carl said.

"But it will be by the time we get home," she pointed out patiently.

"We didn't oversleep today, unlike someone else in the family. We also made it to school on time, too," John said.

"Plus none of us dozed off in class, either," Henry added for good measure.

"All well and good, but you're growing boys and you need your rest. You're going to have a busy weekend ahead, too. You don't want to be all worn-out before you leave."

"We won't be going anywhere this weekend if you don't remember to sign our permission slips," Carl groused, though goodnaturedly. "Tomorrow is the deadline to turn them in. If we don't, we're out of luck."

"Oh, no, I forgot again last night." Eloise shot her sons a rueful glance as Bill herded them into the limousine. "I *promise* I'll sign them as soon as we get home."

"Where are you going on your trip?" Bill asked once they were all settled in the limousine and heading toward Eloise's apartment.

"Washington, D.C. We're leaving from school Friday afternoon and spending the weekend touring the Smithsonian, or at least as many parts of it as we can get to in a couple of days,'' Carl replied.

''It's supposed to be an overview of the museum,'' John explained. ''Then we'll at least have an idea of what's there.''

''Quite a lot,'' Bill said. ''I remember feeling overwhelmed the first time I went. The place is massive. You're definitely going to need a lot of energy.''

''Just like I said,'' Eloise added for good measure.

''Are you going along to chaperone?'' Bill asked, a speculative gleam in his eyes as he turned his gaze her way.

''Not this time,'' she replied. ''I hosted the welcome luncheon for our school volunteers in September so I've done my parental duty for the semester.''

''So you'll be on your own all weekend,'' he continued.

''Yes, actually I will....''

Until that moment, Eloise hadn't really had time to consider what it would be like to have all three sons away for an entire weekend. They had occasionally spent one night at a friend's house. But because there were three of them, she was usually the one who hosted the sleepovers.

She was more used to a group of boys bumping and thumping around the apartment than their friends' parents were, and she really liked it when her sons invited friends to stay over. The more, the merrier had always been her motto where her children were concerned.

Now faced with the prospect of a weekend all alone, she felt oddly let down. It was probably too late to sign on as a chaperone, and knowing her sons and their growing need for independence, they likely wouldn't appreciate it if she did.

She supposed she could use the time to catch up on paperwork. She certainly had enough of that to keep her busy. But she wasn't really looking forward to rattling around her apartment—

"Any plans?" Bill asked, interrupting her reverie.

"Oh, I have lots to do," Eloise answered quickly, meeting his gaze, then glancing away. "Lots and lots to do."

"Mmm…I imagine you do."

Again Bill favored her with a considering look, his tone of voice indicating that he wasn't quite convinced by her avowal.

"Maybe you guys could go on a date or something," Henry suggested, his eyes twinkling.

"Oh, well, I don't think—" Eloise began.

"Now there's an idea I like," Bill cut in. "A date or *something* might be a lot of fun."

Eloise was ready to say that wasn't a good idea at all. Unfortunately no reason came to mind as to why it wasn't. Luckily, though, they arrived just then at her apartment building, and she wasn't required to make an immediate reply.

In the bustle of getting the boys out of the limousine, into the building and onto the elevator, she hoped Bill would let the matter drop. He had to know as well as she that they couldn't be seen as a couple. In fact, they couldn't *be* a couple without having to face possibly dire consequences.

Their differences of opinion over the issue of funding cuts were just too great to be ignored. And she, for one, had too much to lose by even appearing to have gone over to his way of thinking. Who would believe in her, not to mention her cause, if she started dating her personal nemesis at such a crucial and controversial time?

There were still quite a few people living in New York City who wanted funds to continue to be available to help support nonprofit organizations. And she was their spokesperson. She had a responsibility toward them as well as to all those who depended on Manhattan Multiples in various ways.

So engrossed was Eloise in arguing herself out of seeing Bill again socially that she didn't realize her sons had left her alone with him in the hallway outside their apartment. One minute she was walking alongside Bill, her head down, the sound of her sons' voices echoing around her in a familiar way. The next minute she heard a door open then quickly close, and all was silent as the boys went into the apartment without her.

Frowning, she glanced up at Bill.

"They should have at least said thank you and goodnight," she murmured apologetically.

"They did," Bill assured her with a teasing smile. "All three of them. You seemed a little distracted. That's probably why you didn't notice."

"Yes, you're right." She looked away, suddenly uncomfortable.

They were standing together just as they had last night. He had kissed her then. Would he try to kiss her again now? Did she want him to? And, most important of all, would she let him if he did?

She knew she shouldn't, but that didn't necessarily mean she wouldn't. In fact, considering her track record so far—

"You're looking a little distracted again," Bill said, his tone as teasing as the glimmer in his eyes. "What do you have on your mind that's so important? I'd like to think it's something good, but I'm not holding my breath."

"I'm reminding myself that I have to remember to sign those permission slips," she replied, grasping at the first excuse for her inattention that came to mind.

Too late she realized that talk of her sons' impending weekend trip had been the catalyst that had raised the issue of her and Bill going on a date.

"I have a feeling you'll find your sons waiting for you in the entryway, permission slips in hand, when you go inside."

"You're probably right. And I really should do that." She took a step away from him. "I had a lovely time tonight."

"So did I. I've also been thinking we could have a lovely weekend, all alone, just the two of us," he added. "I have a house in the Hamptons. It's small, but it's right on the ocean, and it's very secluded. Not many people know about it—not anyone at all in the press.

"I could pick you up Friday evening. It's not a long drive, and there won't be much traffic heading in that direction this time of year. We could spend some time together out of the public eye, catch up on the past seventeen years, get to be friends again, good friends the way we once were without anyone looking over our shoulders."

Bill paused for an instant and touched a gentle hand to her face.

"Come away with me this weekend, Eloise," he urged. "I promise you won't regret it."

He had spoken so quickly and so convincingly that Eloise's first instinct was to say she'd go with him, no questions asked. But then, given a few moments to collect her thoughts, she immediately began to consider all the reasons why she shouldn't.

Well, actually, the one reason why she shouldn't—

she was already much too attracted to him for her own good. She had loved him once, could all too easily love him again, and that would be as foolhardy now as it had been seventeen years ago.

His political career had been of primary importance to him then, and it still was now. Otherwise he wouldn't be proposing to cut funding for the organization to which she had devoted so much of her life. Her happiness would be more important to him than anything.

"I don't really think—" she began as she had earlier, looking away from his penetrating gaze.

"If the expression on your face is any indication, you're thinking too much," he cut in. "And I have a feeling you're thinking about things that have no relation to us on a personal level. Can't we just be two ordinary people, a man and a woman who enjoy each other's company for one weekend?"

"I'm not sure we can," Eloise admitted.

"Well then, run away with me and let's find out."

"Oh, Bill, I just—"

"Don't give me a definite answer now. Just think about it, okay? I'm going out to my house on Friday, regardless. I'll stop by here for you at seven o'clock. If you want to join me, fine. If not, fine, too."

She wanted to voice a protest of some sort, wanted to tell him not to count on her company, but before she could, he pulled her into his arms and kissed her as thoroughly as he had in his office. And just as she had in his office, Eloise melted against him, welcoming the teasing touch of his tongue to hers with a soft sigh.

She wasn't sure how or why she turned so easily to putty in his hands, but the sad fact was that she did. There was something demanding and commanding about his kisses that she simply couldn't resist. They promised so much of what she wanted and needed in her life but had thought she'd never have again.

Surely she was just lonely, and surely any decent, respectable single man would have assuaged that loneliness just as well. Only she hadn't wanted to kiss any of the other decent, respectable single men she'd met recently. She had wanted to kiss just Bill…just like this.

"Mom, come on, you have to sign our permission slips," Carl said as he opened the door. "We're not going to bed until you do."

"What did I tell you? Standing in the entryway waiting for you. You didn't have to worry about those permission slips at all," Bill murmured in her ear as he broke off their kiss.

"Obviously not," she muttered in agreement.

"See you Friday evening," he added, again for her ears only. Then he winked at Carl. "Have fun in D.C."

"We will, sir. Thank you, and thanks again for tonight."

"Yes, thanks for tonight," Eloise said, not quite meeting his gaze.

"It was my pleasure."

He gave her a last, chaste kiss on the cheek, saluted her sons with a wave of his hand and strode down the hall to the elevator like a man without a care in the world.

"So, do you have a date for the weekend?" Carl asked jauntily, then scurried into the apartment as she shot him a pointed look.

"That is none of your business. Now, where are those permission slips?"

"Right here." Henry waved his above his head.

"Too bad you'll only be gone one weekend."

"Hey, you'd miss us too much if we were gone longer."

"Right now I'm thinking military school might not be such a bad idea after all. Sometimes you guys make me crazy," Eloise groused.

"Hey, that's our job. We're your children."

It seemed to be Bill's job, too, Eloise thought as she sent the boys off to bed with signed permission slips finally in hand.

She couldn't go away with him for the weekend. Well, she could, but she shouldn't. Well, she shouldn't, but she—

She would think about it and decide what to do when she wasn't under the influence of one of his drugging kisses. And she would decide wisely.

Unless, of course, she decided, for once in her life, to throw caution to the wind.

Chapter Six

"So you're still planning to head out to your house in the Hamptons this evening?" Wally Phillips asked.

His tone reflected the same disapproval of the idea he'd avowed since Thursday morning when Bill had first advised his assistant of his plans for the weekend. Several public appearances around the city had had to be canceled, and that had made Wally the one thing he most hated to be—the bearer of bad news.

Though none of the events Bill had been set to attend were high profile, negative fallout, also known as negative publicity, resulting from the mayor's no-show status was always a possibility. Wally worked too hard to present the mayor in a positive light to risk having his image sullied in even the smallest way, especially at such a crucial time for the city.

To be able to say that Bill would make his previously

scheduled public appearances as planned would have made him an extremely happy camper.

But understanding Wally's concerns and acting on them were two very different things. And Bill had already decided Wednesday night that only an all-out state of emergency would cause him to change the plans he had made for the weekend.

"Yes, Wally, I'm still heading out to the Hamptons as planned." He paused and glanced at his watch. "In about thirty minutes to be exact. Even the mayor of New York City deserves a little time off. Or maybe I should say *especially* the mayor of New York City."

"I realize that, sir, but we've always made an effort to schedule your time off well in advance. We've always agreed that was the best way to avoid problems," his assistant said, allowing the slightest hint of impatience to shade his tone.

"And I've stuck to our schedule religiously for the past two years. I've put my mayoral duties first and foremost in my life since my election, and you know it. Now I'm taking one weekend off—*one weekend.* And yes, a few people will be disappointed because I won't be making a personal appearance at their social function, but I refuse to feel guilty about it."

Actually, Bill didn't like having to make last-minute cancellations any more than Wally did, and he regretted causing anyone disappointment. But the choice between attending a couple of minor public engagements and spending an entire weekend alone with Eloise was an easy one to make.

Not that he had any firm reason to believe that she would be waiting for him, bag packed and ready to go, when he arrived at her apartment in less than an hour. But he hadn't given up hope, either. And, as he'd told her after he'd kissed her Wednesday night, he was getting out of town for the next couple of days, with or without her.

He needed a little time away, and while he would prefer to share that time with her, he could also manage on his own quite happily if need be.

"The weather is supposed to be miserable," Wally warned. "Cloudy and cold with a good chance of rain. They're even talking about a possibility of snow overnight Saturday and into Sunday morning. What if you get stuck out there?"

"All the better," Bill replied with a smile.

"For you maybe," Wally groused as he pushed out of his chair. "You have a meeting scheduled with Francis Wegner, President of Construction Services, Monday morning and an interview with Charles Goodwin, the reporter from the *Daily Express,* Monday afternoon."

"Neither of whom will mind a postponement if the weather is so bad that I can't get back to the city to meet with them." Standing, too, Bill gathered the letters he'd been signing during their conversation and handed them to his assistant.

"You're probably right about that," Wally agreed as he tucked the letters into the leather portfolio he carried with him at all times.

"I don't want you working all weekend, either, Wally," Bill said, slipping into his suit jacket then reaching for his overcoat. "Take some time off and do something fun for a change."

"Yeah, sure." Wally smiled slightly, obviously not quite convinced that such an idea was a wise one.

In that instant he reminded Bill much too much of himself at the same age. He had worked days, nights and weekends in pursuit of a political career, leaving little time or energy for anything or anyone else in his life. Had he known then what he knew now, he would have done things differently. He had read somewhere recently that on one's deathbed, one didn't regret not spending more time at the office, but did regret not spending more time with the people one loved.

That statement had made an impression on Bill, lingering in the back of his mind. It was one of the reasons why he'd been so adamant about taking some time off that weekend.

"Seriously, you need to get out more, see your friends, visit your family," Bill urged.

"Is that why you're heading out of town for the weekend? To see friends, or rather, one friend in particular?" Wally asked, leveling a speculative gaze Bill's way. "Ms. Vale, maybe?"

Bill returned his assistant's look with a warning frown.

"I'm not sure that's really any of your business."

"It will be if some photographer snaps a picture of the two of you together and the photo ends up on the front pages of all the papers. I can see the headlines now: 'The Mayor and the Socialite—A Romantic Rendezvous in the Hamptons.'"

"Don't worry, Wally. You won't be seeing any photographs or any lurid headlines in the papers. I may be the mayor of New York City, but I'm also capable of keeping my personal life private whenever necessary. Now let's get out of here so we can enjoy ourselves."

"I have a few things to finish up, sir. See you on Monday?"

"Yes, see you on Monday, weather permitting."

Glad to get away, especially since he was now running late, Bill made his way to the ground floor alone on the elevator. He had arranged for his driver to collect his SUV, already loaded with his overnight bag, from Gracie Mansion, and have it waiting for him outside city hall at six o'clock.

It was now almost six-thirty and he'd told Eloise he would stop by her apartment on his way out of town at seven. He was really going to have to hoof it to make it there on time.

"Hey, Ray, sorry to have kept you waiting so long," he greeted his driver as the man stood beside the SUV, holding the door open for him. "I'm running late as usual."

"No problem, sir. You've got a full tank of gas and air in the tires. Your chef sent along a cooler with sandwiches and soft drinks, too. He figured you'd rather not have to stop along the way to get something to eat."

"Sounds great. Can I drop you anywhere? I'm heading uptown."

"No, sir. I'm meeting some friends for dinner in Chinatown. The restaurant's only a few blocks away and I need the walk." Smiling ruefully, Ray patted his paunch.

"Have a good time, then. And thanks again for being so patient."

"My pleasure, sir. Enjoy the weekend."

"I will. See you Monday."

As Ray strode off with a wave of his hand, Bill climbed into the SUV and started the engine. Alone at last, maneuvering through the Friday-night traffic, thankfully not as heavy as it could have been, he finally allowed himself to consider whether Eloise had decided to go with him or not.

Since offering his spur-of-the-moment invitation Wednesday night, he had made a concerted effort to keep thoughts of the upcoming weekend at bay. He hadn't wanted to jinx his wild and crazy idea of a getaway with Eloise by considering all the reasons why he probably would have been wiser not to.

Nor did he want to consider too closely all the reasons why, in the second place, she would see the foolishness of it for herself and beg off—politely, of course.

He had never been one to act in an especially spontaneous manner. He much preferred to think about all the aspects of a situation before becoming involved. He also liked planning ahead and scheduling activities accordingly whenever possible.

He had no clue as to what had possessed him to suggest Eloise go with him to his house in the Hamptons for the weekend. More than likely it had been the aching need to be with her in a place where they could have some private time together—a need that had consumed him since he'd kissed her the night of the Mayor's Ball.

But he had rarely, if ever, acted on such a primal feeling in his life. Only now was he realizing what a mistake that had probably been. But then, only Eloise had ever stirred such a strong desire in him, and she had chosen to marry someone else seventeen years ago.

Now she was free, however, and so was he. They were older, too, and he, for one, was wiser about the difference between merely wanting someone and needing them in a viscerally unrelenting way. He also knew better than to ignore any opportunity to be with her, especially when such opportunities could be so fleeting.

In a perfect world he would have been able to win back Eloise's affection slowly over a more reasonable period of time before offering to take her away for a weekend. But they didn't live in a perfect world.

He had commitments he couldn't avoid fulfilling, and so did she. She also had three teenage sons who rightly demanded a big chunk of her time and attention. There wouldn't be many occasions when he'd have a chance to be alone with her. To pass one by would be a big mistake.

He had acted on instinct to spur the attraction he'd sensed between them at the Mayor's Ball on Tuesday night and again following the basketball game Wednesday. And instinct had told him that he'd lose Eloise all over again unless he let her know, unequivocally, just how much she had always meant to him.

But would she cooperate?

The question had haunted him for the past two days, lingering in the back of his mind every waking moment he'd had since leaving her at her front door Wednesday evening. She had all but refused his invitation outright when he'd first extended it. Only his timely interjections had kept open the possibility that she would change her mind and opt to come with him tonight.

That and the fact that she hadn't called yesterday or today to tell him she'd made other plans.

So there was still a good chance she was waiting for him, packed and ready to go. And probably tapping her foot, wondering where the heck he was, Bill thought as he cast an eye on the dashboard clock and saw that it was almost 7:10.

He could call her on his cell phone and let her know he was running late, but he'd be there in another ten minutes at the most. And he would rather have her send him away in person than to be told not to stop by over the phone. If that was what she intended to do.

He'd go off alone then, just as he'd planned. He hadn't been kidding about needing some time to unwind. And left to his own devices, he'd also have a chance to plan several alternate ways in which to ease himself into Eloise's life once again.

It wouldn't be a simple task. The funding cut issue loomed between them as a major irreconcilable difference—one she seemed determined to remind him of on a regular basis. And once the cuts had actually been made, as they would be, her animosity toward him could increase considerably.

Unless he first convinced her that she mattered to him, personally, she might not allow him anywhere near her again. He knew that caring about the good of the city didn't preclude his caring about her well-being and that of her organization. But she could assume that was the case all too easily if he didn't make sure she knew differently. And the upcoming weekend would provide him with the chance to do just that.

At exactly 7:20 Bill pulled up in front of Eloise's apartment. He pulled the Official City Business placard from the glove box of the SUV and positioned it on the dashboard. The last thing he needed was to be issued a parking ticket outside her building.

Drawing a breath, he opened the door and stepped outside. A gust of cold, damp air slipped under the collar of his coat and sent a chill down his neck as he hurried to the double glass doors, one of which the doorman held open for him.

He blamed the icy blast for the tiny tremor that momentarily shook his hands. He had stopped being anxious about most things years ago. Though maybe it was more that he hadn't had a reason to be anxious for a very long time, and now he finally did.

Eloise paced slowly from one end of her living room to the other just as she'd been doing for almost thirty

minutes. Busier than usual at work both Thursday and
Friday, not to mention thoroughly caught up in helping
her sons pack for their trip to Washington, D.C., last
night, she hadn't had time earlier to be nervous about
the weekend ahead. She was now making up for it in
spades.

She had come home by way of the boys' school so
she could wave them off with the other parents as they'd
boarded the chartered bus. Arriving at her apartment just
before six o'clock, she had hurriedly tossed a pair of
wool pants, a couple of shirts and sweaters, socks, un-
derwear and toiletries into her overnight bag. She had
zipped it up and set it in the foyer along with her navy-
blue down parka, matching gloves and cashmere scarf,
then headed for the bathroom to take a quick shower.
Makeup freshened and hair brushed, she had dressed in
clean jeans, a denim shirt, black wool V-neck sweater,
warm wool socks and low-heeled, lace-up black boots.

Hopefully just the right attire for a casual winter
weekend at the beach, she thought as she paused before
an ornately framed oval mirror ånd studied her reflection. That is, if she was actually going to have a casual
winter weekend at the beach.

Glancing at the clock on the mantel, she saw that it
was not quite seven-fifteen—late, but not extremely so.
Except that Bill Harper had always been punctual to a
fault. Which might very well mean he wasn't coming at
all.

Her stomach tense and her mouth dry, Eloise turned
away from the mirror and walked to the kitchen for a
glass of water.

She wasn't sure if she was more anxious about the
possibility that Bill would eventually arrive as promised
or the equally disquieting possibility that he had actually

taken her at her word Wednesday night and had written off their weekend together as a no-go proposition.

Of course, she could have spared herself such worry easily enough. She could have followed through on her initial attempt to refuse his invitation by calling his office and leaving a firmly stated message for him. Or she could have called his office to let him know she was looking forward to seeing him Friday evening as planned. Problem was, she hadn't decided what to do until an hour ago.

Those few moments when she'd allowed herself to consider Bill's offer of a weekend getaway, she mostly came up with reasons why she shouldn't go to the Hamptons with him. But those reasons, all valid under the circumstances, hadn't been enough to quell completely the desire deep within her to do exactly what he'd asked—spend some time alone with him, enjoying his company, as he seemed to want to enjoy hers, for one measly little weekend.

Just like any sane woman would do without the slightest hesitation, if offered such an opportunity by the man she loved.

She was most certainly sane—at least as sane as anyone she knew. And as Bill had pointed out Wednesday night, she had as much right as he did to set aside certain issues temporarily, no matter how divisive those issues might be, for the sake of her own personal happiness.

Only the thought of the price that might have to be paid by others had held her back. That is, until she'd walked into her big, empty and all-too-silent apartment just before six o'clock that evening.

Choosing between a weekend alone in her penthouse and a weekend with Bill at his Hamptons house had suddenly become a no-brainer. She had willingly made many sacrifices for the benefit of Manhattan Multiples, and she would willingly make many more. But she wasn't going to add giving up time alone with Bill Harper to the list.

Although she may have already done just that Wednesday night by the simple act of speaking without really considering the consequences—

The shrill ring of the telephone startled Eloise so much that she almost dropped her glass in the sink. Any calls concerning the boys would have come through on her cell phone. That was the number she'd left with the school in case of an emergency. Bill was the only one she could think of who would be trying to contact her at her home number, and then most likely only to confirm that he wouldn't be stopping by to pick her up, after all.

Her spirits sinking, Eloise managed to set her glass on the counter, then reached for the wall unit's receiver and offered as cheerful a greeting as she could manage.

''Oh, good, you're home,'' her assistant Allison Baker Perez said.

''Allison? Is something wrong?''

Her relief that Bill wasn't the one calling was immediately overshadowed by concern for the younger woman. She couldn't remember her assistant ever calling her at home on a Friday evening. In fact, she couldn't recall Allison contacting her at home unless a major problem concerning something to do with Manhattan Multiples had arisen.

''Not at all. I…we…Jorge and I were wondering if you might like to have dinner with us. That is, if you haven't made other plans. We could pick you up in twenty minutes or so. Nothing fancy—pizza maybe, or Chinese food, or burgers and fries. You're welcome to choose. It's just that I thought of you home alone all weekend and maybe feeling lonely with the boys away…'' Allison's voice trailed off on a questioning note, then she added before Eloise had a chance to reply, ''I'll…we'll understand if you'd rather not.''

''Allison, how kind of you and Jorge to think of me and include me in your plans for the evening,'' Eloise said.

Her heart warmed by her assistant's caring consideration, she didn't even hesitate before deciding to accept her invitation.

''I'd love to—'' she began, then was cut off by the buzz of the intercom. ''Can you hold on a second, Allison?''

''Sure.''

Eloise pushed the appropriate button to put Allison's call on hold, then answered the doorman's summons.

''Yes, Carlton?''

''Ms. Vale, Mayor Harper is here. Shall I send him upstairs?''

''Yes…yes, of course,'' she replied, her tummy fluttering.

He had stopped by for her as promised after all. Later than she would have ever expected him to be, but he was here all the same, to her slightly giddy delight.

She clicked on the telephone line again and tried to keep the sudden excitement out of her voice as she spoke to Allison once more.

''As I was saying, I'd love to join you and Jorge for dinner, but I've made plans already. Maybe another time?''

''Oh, yes, any other time would be fine,'' Allison readily agreed. ''Maybe after I've had my sonogram…''

''Which you've scheduled for next Thursday, right?''

"Yes, next Thursday. We'll know then if I'm having a multiple birth, won't we?"

"I don't know about you, sweetie, but I'm pretty sure already. Have you mentioned the possibility to Jorge yet?"

"I thought maybe we could have done that at dinner tonight," Allison admitted, a trace of anxiety in her voice.

"He'll be thrilled," Eloise assured her. "At least he will be once the initial shock has worn off. Your instincts are on target, too. Better to prepare him for the possibility before you have the sonogram. Make sure he has a beer with his pizza tonight, then tell him what you suspect. Then prepare to be even more coddled that you are already."

"Eloise, what would I do without you and Manhattan Multiples?"

"You would do just fine, sweetie, but I'm glad I can be a part of your support group."

"A part of it? You're so much more than that. You're a wonderful friend and mentor," Allison insisted.

"Thanks for thinking of me that way. You've been a wonderful friend to me, too, and a huge asset to Manhattan Multiples. I couldn't have asked for a better personal assistant than you've been to me." Eloise smiled despite the mist of tears in her eyes, then felt her tummy flutter again as the door chimes sounded. "I have to go now. See you Monday."

"Unless we're snowed in," Allison replied with a hint of laughter in her voice.

"Snowed in?" Eloise repeated, making no effort to hide her dismay.

She hadn't paid much attention to the weather reports

the past few days mostly because she hadn't taken the time to watch any of the nightly network news shows.

"It's in the forecast for the weekend," Allison explained.

"Oh, dear…"

"Have fun tonight, Eloise. Bye."

"Bye…"

Eloise cradled the receiver, then spun on her heel and hurried to the foyer to answer the door. Her mind whirled with at least half a dozen heretofore unthought-of reasons why going out to the Hamptons with Bill might not be such a good idea after all.

At the very top of her list was the possibility that they might not be able to get back to the city Sunday night. Then what would happen?

A frown furrowing her forehead, she opened the door and met Bill's steady gaze. His eyes were alight with excitement, and there was a boyishness about his smile that touched her soul. Seeing the look on her face, though, his expression quickly changed to one of concern.

"Is something wrong—aside from the fact that I'm almost thirty minutes late?" he asked. "And very sorry for that, I might add."

"I didn't know it was supposed to snow this weekend," she answered, then shot him a rueful smile. "And, yes, you are late, and you're never late, ever. I'd just about given up on you."

"So which of those statements explains the ominous frown you had on your face when you opened the door?"

His grin in place again, he joined her in the foyer as she held the door wide in invitation.

"All both," she said, making him laugh.

"As I said, I'm sorry I'm late. Begging and pleading with my assistant to let me have the weekend off took me a little longer than I'd anticipated. And don't worry about the threat of snow. I think the local weathermen like to terrorize us with worst-case scenarios. We'll probably have a few flurries at the most, and since my SUV has four-wheel drive, we can get through a lot more than that, if necessary."

"I was just concerned about getting home before the boys return from their trip to D.C."

"I can almost guarantee you will be. But if something should happen to prevent it, I'll see that they're well taken care of until you're home again. How's that sound?"

"Reassuring," she admitted.

"So, does that mean you've decided to run away with me for the weekend?"

"I know I should have called to let you know for sure, but I didn't make up my mind until an hour or so ago. And yes, I've decided to run away with you for the weekend. I'm all packed and everything." She waved a hand at her overnight bag as she grabbed her jacket.

"No problem," Bill quipped, his grin widening as he helped her into her jacket. "I really enjoy having a sleepless night every now and then."

"Very funny." She shot him a wry glance, then added, "I'll be right back. I want to make sure the timers on the lights are set."

Her heart soaring with the kind of girlish anticipation she hadn't felt in years, Eloise quickly made a last tour of the apartment. Returning to the foyer, she met Bill's gaze as he stood quietly, one hand holding the handle of her overnight bag, the other tucked comfortably into the pocket of his overcoat.

There was a searching look in his eyes now, and his grin had softened into an inquiring smile that lent him an odd air of uncertainty. In someone who had always seemed to her so sure of himself, not to mention so sure of everything he said and did, even this slight hint of insecurity was exquisitely endearing.

He was human after all, with many of the same doubts she and so many other people suffered when they began a close personal relationship with someone special. He might be the mayor of New York City, but he was no more confident than she of how their weekend together would progress. For some strange reason she found that reassuring.

"Ready?" he asked after a last moment of hesitation.

"As I'll ever be," she replied, gathering her purse, keys, scarf and gloves from the entryway table.

The nervousness had changed to eager expectation. And much to her chagrin, somewhere in the back of her mind the words to a familiar winter song repeated over and over as they walked down the hallway to the waiting elevator.

Let it snow, let it snow, let it snow…

Chapter Seven

Having tucked Eloise comfortably into the front passenger seat of his SUV, Bill walked around to the driver's side door. Then, and only then, was he hit by the realization that he was about to have the only woman he'd ever loved all to himself for two days and two nights. Whatever he said and whatever he did during that time was going to make all the difference as to how the rest of his life unfolded. And for once in his life he hadn't plotted and planned exactly how to proceed.

Of course, he'd seen to many of the basic physical details necessary to make his normally unoccupied house a cozy, comfortable place to stay. He had called the couple who served as caretakers in his absence and asked them to air the linens in both the master bedroom and the guest bedroom, to stock the refrigerator with fresh food and stack firewood at the ready by the back door.

But he hadn't thought about what he wanted to say to

Eloise simply because he hadn't been sure he'd have the opportunity to share his thoughts and feelings with her, after all.

Now he was about to embark on a journey with her that could make all the difference in his life. What he said and what he did over the next couple of days and nights would either draw them closer than he'd ever allowed himself to believe possible, or split them apart once and for all. He could make any number of unfortunate if not fatal mistakes that might result in their relationship ending before it had even really begun.

As he reached for the door handle, Bill noted again the slight tremor in his hand. He had wanted only to relax and enjoy the weekend ahead with Eloise, but the tension suddenly coursing through him made that goal seem unrealistic, at least just then.

He settled himself behind the steering wheel and slid the key in the ignition, started the engine, then finally looked over at Eloise. She returned his gaze, her smile seeming more tentative than it had earlier.

Was she, too, wondering what she'd gotten herself into by accepting his invitation? Was she, in fact, regretting her decision already? Was she wishing there were some way she could change her mind before he pulled away from the curb and drove off into the night?

Though Bill couldn't quite bring himself to ask those questions aloud, he didn't immediately shift the SUV into gear. He took off his gloves and scarf and tossed them onto the back seat, allowing the silence to stretch between them almost painfully. He put his hands on the steering wheel and stared out the windshield for a few seconds, then glanced at Eloise again.

She sat in the passenger seat, her attention seemingly focused on her own gloves and scarf, now neatly folded in her lap. She smoothed a hand over them again and again as if seeking some sort of reassurance.

He looked away again uncertainly, and as he did, the small thermal cooler on the back seat caught his eye.

"Are you hungry?" he asked, then added before she had a chance to reply, "Because Ray, my driver, mentioned that Dennis, my chef, packed sandwiches and soft drinks for us. Nothing fancy, I'm sure. Probably his chicken salad stuffed in whole-wheat pita bread. Dennis knows that's my favorite."

Eloise hesitate only a moment, then smiled at him with obvious relief.

"Actually, I *am* hungry, and I love chicken salad stuffed into whole-wheat pita bread, too."

"Do you mind if we eat while I drive?"

"Not at all."

Relieved himself, Bill returned her smile for just an instant. Then he leaned over the seat to retrieve the cooler and set it on the console between them where it fit securely.

Inside the cooler, topped with a couple of cloth napkins, he found not only a sandwich and soft drink for each of them, but also half a dozen brownies individually wrapped and zipped into a plastic baggie.

"Oh, wow, this looks good," Eloise said as she carefully unwrapped her chicken-salad-stuffed pita pocket.

"It's amazing what Dennis can do with a little chopped chicken and some fresh vegetables," Bill agreed.

He set their soft drinks in the cup holders and set his own sandwich on the console for easy access while Eloise moved the cooler to the floor by her feet.

"Mmm, you're right—amazing," she said a moment later after taking a bite of her sandwich.

"Wait till you try the brownies. You'll be swooning with delight," he advised as he finally put the SUV into gear.

Pulling away from the curb, he carefully guided the vehicle into the flow of traffic before he sampled his own sandwich.

"Good thing I kept the cooler handy."

"Only if you plan to share."

"Of course I'll share." Eloise grinned at him again as she reached for her soft drink. "I'm not a total oinker."

"You're not an oinker at all," Bill assured her, finally feeling able to relax, if not completely, then close enough to make the drive to the Hamptons a pleasurable experience.

"I would be if I ate all those brownies myself."

"You might still be tempted once you taste one."

"I'll have you know I rarely let temptation get in the way of good manners. And it wouldn't be mannerly of me to eat all the brownies no matter how scrumptious they are."

"Ah, yes, good manners are important, aren't they, Ms. Vale?" he quipped in return.

"Very important, Mr. Mayor. Without good manners one might be tempted to behave in all sorts of wanton ways."

"And behaving in all sorts of wanton ways is a bad thing?"

"Sometimes yes and sometimes no. Depends on the situation," she conceded, sending him a suddenly shy smile that had his pulse racing in an unexpected way.

"So I'll definitely get my share of the brownies?"

"That I can promise you for sure. Anything else…" She lifted her shoulders in an elegant shrug, then took another bite of her sandwich as she eyed the line of cars ahead of them waiting for the light at the corner to change. "The traffic doesn't seem too bad, or maybe I should say it doesn't seem as bad as I thought it would be."

Accepting the change of subject easily enough, Bill agreed with her.

"It's not bad at all compared to summer. With luck we should be out of the worst of the stop-and-go in another ten blocks or so. I'm guessing we'll be at the house by nine-thirty or ten o'clock at the latest."

"Sounds good to me."

They finished their sandwiches in silence as Bill maneuvered the SUV through the gradually thinning traffic. Eloise then got out the brownies, setting the plastic baggie on the console within easy reach of each of them and taking one of the rich chocolate squares for herself.

Her ensuing sigh of delight made Bill laugh.

"Told you so," he said.

"You did, indeed," she agreed, then added with an encouraging smile. "Now tell me about your house. I've been trying to imagine what it's like the past couple days, but it's been hard."

"What do you want to know about it?" Bill, too, helped himself to a brownie as he waited for her reply.

"Anything and everything you want to tell me."

"That could take an awfully long time."

"Then just the facts for now."

"Okay—the facts."

He hesitated a moment, organizing his thoughts. He loved his little beachfront house, and he wanted Eloise to love it, too. But it wasn't anything special—at least not in comparison to most houses in the Hamptons. He wasn't sure how much size and style would matter to her. Probably not a lot, if he was any judge of character, but still, Eloise had gotten used to the finer things in life over the past seventeen years.

"It's really more of a cottage," he advised her at last. "A real, old-fashioned cottage, too. Not one of those overblown, multilevel, multiroom monstrosities the rich and famous like to refer to as cottages. There's one big room downstairs that includes a kitchen, dining alcove and living room with fireplace. The wall facing the ocean is made up of floor-to-ceiling windows and a pair of French doors that open onto a wood deck. Upstairs there are two bedrooms, each about the same size and each with a small but private bathroom."

"Oh, Bill, it sounds lovely."

"I think it is," he admitted. "Although it was in pretty bad shape when I bought it fifteen years ago. Of course, that's probably why I could afford it in the first place.

"I worked on it religiously every chance I had and I'm proud to say it's now totally livable. The kitchen is small, but state-of-the-art, the bathrooms are completely modernized with hot water on tap at all times, the wood floors are sanded and polished, and the walls are freshly painted.

"The furnishings are a bit sparse, but there are enough chairs, tables and beds, not to mention a big leather sofa in front of the fireplace, to make it reasonably comfortable. Although that's just my opinion since I don't entertain there often. Well, actually, not at all, so all I can say for sure is that I'm comfortable when I'm there and I hope you will be, too."

"I can't imagine why I wouldn't," Eloise assured him with a sweet, soft smile. "I'm not really all that demanding. I didn't grow up living in the lap of luxury, you know.'' She quirked an eyebrow at him. ''We never did talk much about our pre-New York City lives, did we?''

''I remember you told me you grew up in a suburb of St. Louis.''

''An extremely middle-class suburb. I never expected to end up living in a penthouse apartment on Park Avenue when I first moved to New York. And while I admit it's quite nice, I could do with a lot less and be just as happy if I had to. Although I doubt I ever will, thanks to Walter's forethought. He made sure the boys and I would always be financially secure.''

''I'm glad of that,'' Bill said as he turned off the expressway. ''And I wasn't insinuating that you're a snob. I just wanted to be sure you knew my cottage really was just a cottage.''

Reaching out, he gave her hand a squeeze, and she flashed him a grateful smile in return.

''I wouldn't mind if it was a one-room shack as long as it's warm and dry.''

''It's definitely not a one-room shack, and it will definitely be warm and dry when we get there.''

''Well, then, what's not to like?''

''Amazing…''

''What?''

''How agreeable you can be.''

''Of course I can be agreeable…about some things,'' she replied, a hint of tartness in her voice.

Aware that Eloise might think he was attempting to steer their conversation toward certain issues—something he was most certainly determined not to do that weekend—Bill raised one hand in a placating gesture.

''I didn't mean to sound accusatory,'' he said. ''I was only talking about your amenable disposition toward the so-far sight-unseen-by-you accommodations I'm providing for the weekend.''

"Oh, well, then…no offense taken.'' She sketched a seemingly diffident shrug as she glanced at him.

"Good.''

Again he reached across the console to give her hand a reassuring squeeze. To his relief, she returned the gentle pressure, her expression lightening once more.

"Can we agree to a truce of sorts for the duration of the weekend where certain differences of opinion are concerned?'' she asked shyly after a few moments.

"We most certainly can,'' he agreed, glad that she had voiced his own hope for the two days they had ahead of them.

"So tell me then, do you get out to your cottage often?''

"Not nearly often enough,'' Bill admitted. "At least not since being elected mayor. Hardly anyone knows I own a Hamptons house, and since I'd like to keep it that way, hanging out there during high season has been out of the question. I mostly head out there when anyone with any sense would be content to stay in the city.''

"Like a rainy weekend in November with a chance of snow in the forecast?''

"Exactly.'' He flashed a grin at her as he switched on the windshield wipers to clear the glass of a sudden smattering of droplets.

They rode along in companionable silence for a few minutes, then he continued on another track.

"I'm assuming the boys got off on their trip without any hitches.''

"I waved them off as they boarded the bus at their school. I'm not sure they were glad that I came to say goodbye, but most of the other parents were there, too, so if they were embarrassed, they had lots of company.''

''Thirteen is a hard age. They're not quite young adults, but at the same time they're too grown up to still be considered little children.''

''Tell me about it.'' Eloise uttered a soft sigh. ''Some days I'm astonished at how smart and savvy they seem to be. Other times their behavior is so juvenile I'm sorry I got rid of the little chairs I used to use for time-out.''

Bill couldn't help but laugh at the image of Eloise's three tall, lanky sons lined up in a row, sitting on little kid chairs as a timer ticked away the minutes till their punishment was over.

''They really are very nice young men,'' he said when she favored him with a wry smile. ''You've done a great job raising them.''

''So far, so good,'' she replied.

''You know, I didn't even think to give you the phone number at the cottage so you could leave it with the school in case of an emergency.''

''No problem. They have my cell phone number. Just remind me to plug it into the charger when we get to the cottage.''

''Which should be in five minutes or less,'' Bill advised.

He turned off the two-lane blacktop road that had first taken them past rows of shops, stores, restaurants and closely spaced houses, then patches of woods and an occasional open field, and onto an unmarked sand-and-gravel lane just wide enough to accommodate his SUV. Since leaving the business district, they had passed few other vehicles on the road, probably due to the rain now falling steadily.

Ahead half a mile or so, he could see the faint flicker

of lights through the thick stand of trees that provided privacy, and felt a sense of homecoming.

"You weren't exaggerating when you said your place was secluded," Eloise commented. "Although it's not really all that far from town, is it?"

"Only about fifteen minutes, twenty at the most on a night like tonight."

As he pulled into the clearing past the last stand of trees, and the cottage came fully into view, Eloise drew an audible breath that seemed to express exactly his own feeling of pleasure at seeing his little house, lit enchantingly from within, standing sturdily amidst the wind-whipped sea grass.

"Oh, Bill it's just…lovely," she murmured as he stopped the SUV close to the little flagstone walkway that led to the wide covered porch and the front door beyond.

"It's your basic gingerbread house—white clapboard with black shutters on the windows, front door painted red. The porch wraps around the front and sides, but out back, overlooking the beach, there's the deck I mentioned earlier," he explained.

"I can't wait to see it in the daylight, although it might be covered with snow by then," she teased.

"I don't think it's cold enough for that yet. But if it is, we can stay bundled up inside, warm and dry. I have a couple who keep an eye on the place for me. I called them yesterday and had them air out the bedrooms, turn on the heat, stock the fridge and set the timers on the lights so we could find our way inside without tripping over anything when we got here."

"Perfect planning," Eloise said, looking away quickly, seeming to retreat, if only incrementally.

For a moment Bill wondered if he'd said something

wrong, but he couldn't think what it might have been. More than likely, Eloise had simply started to feel sleepy. He was sure she'd had just as long and hard a day at work as he. That, followed by a long drive on a cold, wet winter night would be enough to tire anyone out. And he remembered her sons teasing her about needing a good night's rest to function well.

"Let's get you settled inside the house. Then I can bring in our bags. How does that sound?" he asked.

"Like an excellent idea," she agreed, though she still seemed somewhat subdued.

Hoping it was only weariness rather than second thoughts that had caused her sudden shift in mood, Bill switched off the SUV's engine. Then he retrieved a fold-up umbrella he kept handy in the console between the seats.

"Hang on a minute and I'll make sure you don't get too wet on the way to the porch."

"Always the gentlemen," she murmured.

"Hey, I try my best...."

With the help of his umbrella, and by putting a guiding arm around her shoulders and keeping her close to his side, Bill got Eloise to the front porch in a reasonably dry state.

She went along with him willingly enough, even giggling a little as they sloshed through a puddle. But once they reached the porch and he slid the key into the door lock, she took a purposeful step away from him.

He shot her a questioning look as he pushed the door open, but she chose not to meet his gaze as she walked across the threshold. Wiping the soles of her wet boots on the multicolored rag rug just inside the tiny entryway, she looked through the archway that opened into the living room and drew another audible breath.

"It really is charming, Bill...really, really charming."

"I was hoping you'd like it."

"Oh, I do. I most certainly do."

She walked into the large open room, her head turning one way, then the other, as she took in the living room, the small but modern kitchen and the dining alcove. She stopped only when she reached the wall of windows with a neatly centered pair of French doors. Though she put her face close to one of the panes of glass, her hands cupped on either side, he knew she wouldn't be able to see much in the rain-shrouded darkness outside.

"The house is set on a slight rise above the dune line," he explained. "The deck is built out to the edge of the rise, then there's a short flight of steps down to a little wooden walkway that crosses the dunes and angles down to the beach."

"The vista looking out these windows must be beautiful in daylight."

"It is, even on a gray and cloudy day. And it's cozier in here when there's a fire in the fireplace. I could light one now," he offered.

Again he sensed a certain hesitation in Eloise—an unexpected drawing back behind a wall of reserve suddenly but surely erected in the time since he'd pulled to a stop in front of the cottage.

"Actually, I'm kind of tired," she said, plucking nervously at the zipper on her jacket as she looked everywhere but at him.

Ever so slowly, realization dawned on Bill. Eloise must not have considered what the sleeping arrangements would be until they'd actually arrived at the cottage. And once she had, she must have experienced a strong sense of discomfort.

He hadn't brought up the subject himself, as he probably should have, because he'd assumed that tonight, at least, and maybe even tomorrow night she would prefer to have a room—and a bed—all to herself.

He hadn't brought her to his house for the express purpose of seducing her. His only real intent had been to renew the friendship they'd shared for all too short a time seventeen years ago.

"You know, now that we're here, so am I," he said. "Must be the weather."

"Must be."

She smiled at him distantly, then went back to fiddling with the zipper on her jacket. She hadn't made any move to take it off despite the steady flow of warm air coming through the vents and heating the cottage to a comfortable level.

"Make yourself at home for a few minutes while I get our bags out of the SUV. Then I'll take you upstairs to the guest room."

For just an instant Eloise finally met his gaze, but Bill wasn't sure if the expression he saw in her eyes was one of relief or regret. Possibly a combination of the two, he decided as he flashed her a grin, then turned to head outside again.

She wasn't completely immune to his charms, after all. But she obviously didn't want to be rushed, either. And after waiting seventeen years to have her back in his life again, he certainly wasn't about to scare her off with caveman tactics.

The rain had intensified to a steady downpour, but the air temperature still seemed to be well above freezing. Trying not to get too wet in the process, Bill took their bags from the back of the SUV and returned to the house.

Inside again, he was glad to see that Eloise had taken

off her jacket. But she still held it clasped to her chest along with her purse, gloves and scarf as she studied the books lining the shelves of the built-in bookcase on one side of the fireplace.

"It really is miserable out there," he said, setting their bags down in the entryway so he could remove his own coat and hang it on the coatrack next to the door.

"Still raining?"

"Harder than ever, but it hasn't gotten any colder." He gestured toward the kitchen area. "Want a cup of tea, or coffee, or maybe cocoa before we go upstairs?"

"No, thanks."

"Come on, then. I'll get you settled in your room."

He lifted the bags again and led the way to the narrow wooden staircase positioned on the far side of the living room. Eloise followed behind him wordlessly, her tread light. At the top of the stairs he gestured with a turn of his shoulder to the first open doorway.

"My room," he said, dropping his bag just across the threshold, then moving down the hallway. "And yours."

He stepped just inside the doorway, paused and set her bag down as he made a visual survey to assure himself that the bedroom she'd be using was in order. Eloise paused beside him, looking around the room, as well.

"What do you think? Will it do?"

"Very nicely, thank you," she replied. "I love the quilt on the bed."

"There's a down blanket underneath it, too, so you should be nice and warm." He waved a hand to the open doorway in the far wall. "The bathroom is through there—fresh towels in the cabinets—just help yourself. I hope you'll be comfortable."

"I'm sure I will."

She moved to stand by one of the two windows framing either side of the bed and again attempted to look out through the wide slats on the blinds.

"The windows face the ocean," he said. "Most mornings the sunrise can be pretty spectacular, although I'm not counting on that being the case tomorrow."

"Me, neither, but maybe the rain will let up."

"Yes, maybe it will."

He hesitated a moment longer. He was torn between the urge to go to her and kiss her at least one time before leaving her alone and the knowledge that one kiss wouldn't be nearly enough for him.

In fact, stopping after sharing only one kiss with her would be impossible. And the last thing he wanted was to frighten her or upset her in any way and risk spoiling the rest of their weekend together. So he stayed where he was in the bedroom doorway and wished her a heartfelt good-night.

"You sleep well, too, Bill," she replied, casting him a last shy glance that he found hard to read.

Again he sensed that she was feeling both relieved and oddly regretful. Had he been just a tad more confident he would have dismissed the one and acted on the other. He'd kissed Eloise twice already and she hadn't minded it either time. But they hadn't been quite so alone, and the circumstances hadn't been quite so amenable to the intensifying of their intimacy as they now happened to be.

And when all was said and done, he was too much of a gentleman to ever take a lady anywhere she was the slightest bit hesitant to go. Especially a lady whom he held in such high regard as he did Eloise, and from whom he wanted to earn an equally high amount of regard in return.

"I'm an early riser, but there's no need for you to get up at the crack of dawn unless you want to," he added.

"Okay."

"And if you're hungry later, or thirsty, just help yourself to anything you want from the kitchen."

"Okay."

"Well then, I'll see you in the morning."

"Yes…see you in the morning, Bill."

"Oh, and be sure to plug in your cell phone so the battery won't go dead."

"Thanks for reminding me. I will."

He backed out of the bedroom, pulling the door closed as he went. The shy smile she'd shot his way with her final "okay" lingered in his mind as he went downstairs again to make a last check of the cottage, lock the front door and switch off the lights.

He was an intelligent, well-educated man, a skilled politician, at ease in almost any social setting or situation. But as he paused in the kitchen, took a glass from one cabinet and a bottle of brandy from another, he felt like a bashful, gangly teenager, clueless in the throes of first love.

Bashful, gangly and clueless he wasn't. As for being in the throes of first love…that was actually true. Eloise had been the first love of his life, and seventeen years later she remained the one and only woman he'd ever really loved.

Maybe this time he would get things right with her, though. Maybe this time he'd find a way to finally win her love in return.

Chapter Eight

Eloise awoke slowly, lured from a deep, peaceful sleep by the scent of coffee brewing and bacon frying. Her stomach growled as she took in the watery daylight filtering through the wide-slatted blinds on the windows.

She had opened them before retiring for the night, hoping—despite all predictions to the contrary—that there would be sunlight to help her welcome the morning. But the bedroom was much too dimly lit at almost eight o'clock for the sky to be anything but gray and cloudy.

At least the rain had stopped, she noted as she snuggled more deeply into the warmth provided by the down blanket under which she'd slept. Or at least it had let up enough so that it no longer tapped forcefully against the windowpanes as it had during most of the night.

Although she really had been as tired as she'd led Bill to believe she was, sleep hadn't come easily. And she had awakened at least twice after she'd eventually dozed off. But always the steady beat of the rain had soothed her back to restfulness, calming the turmoil in her mind and easing the anxiety in her heart and soul.

She had made the decision to go away with Bill for the weekend in a truly cavalier manner. Bottom line, she hadn't wanted to face the prospect of spending two days and nights alone in her apartment. Taking Bill up on his offer of a getaway had seemed a viable alternative.

Renewing his acquaintance at the Mayor's Ball and again at the basketball game had been a gratifying experience. She had also enjoyed his company on the drive to his cottage. He was an intelligent, charming and entertaining companion. She'd had no problem relaxing with him because he'd made it easy.

But then they'd arrived at their destination and apprehension had suddenly replaced her sense of repose. Seeing the secluded place where they would be spending the next two days, and nights, alone together had triggered all sorts of questions and concerns she knew she should have addressed a whole heck of a lot sooner.

No mention had been made of their sleeping arrangements, and she hadn't really thought to ask. Had her acceptance of his invitation led Bill to believe that she would share his bed?

Momentarily taken aback by the prospect, Eloise had realized that she'd have to put some distance between them, albeit in the coolest, firmest, most polite manner she could muster, or suffer the consequences of her earlier disregard.

Although, in all honesty, she doubted there would be any suffering at all involved in sharing Bill Harper's bed. In fact, the thought had actually begun to take on a very definite appeal just about the time he'd ever so coolly,

firmly and politely offered to show her to the cottage's
guest bedroom.

Again Eloise had experienced a sense of dismay, but
at an even more intense level and for a completely different reason altogether.

Obviously Bill hadn't planned to have her share his
bed, and perverse as it had suddenly seemed to her, she'd
been unaccountably yet thoroughly miffed by the time
he'd finally excused himself and left her all alone.

She had known how unfair it was of her to put him
in a damned-if-he-did, damned-if-he-didn't situation.
But she hadn't been able to help it. What did he really
want from her—friendship only, or something much
more intimate and intense? He hadn't kissed her as if he
only wanted her as a friend. But then he'd left her to
sleep alone as if he did.

What was a woman to do? she wondered as she finally
pushed back the bedcovers. The answer came to her almost at once—follow your heart. She had never gone
wrong using that tactic in the past, and she could only
hope she wouldn't now.

Bill had to have sensed her withdrawal when they'd
arrived at the cottage. He had to have been aware of her
sudden hesitation and her all-too-obvious uncertainty.
She'd made no effort to hide her changing emotions, and
he had always been a savvy man. Instead of raging at
him mentally for being wise enough to comprehend her
unspoken concerns and act accordingly in a gentlemanly
fashion, she should be grateful.

He wasn't going to force her into doing anything she
didn't want to do. Instead he was going to wait patiently
for her to lead the way to the kind of relationship she
wanted them to share. All she had to do was make a
decision one way or another and stay with it.

Pausing to look out the window at the misty gray day, dark sky blending almost seamlessly with dark ocean waters, Eloise acknowledged that was one thing easier said than done.

She had so many factors to consider, so many possible pitfalls that she couldn't really ignore. She had too many people depending on her and Manhattan Multiples. She couldn't afford to behave immoderately because there would be serious consequences to pay.

Again, somewhere in the back of her mind *Follow your heart* whispered softly.

The combined aromas of coffee and bacon, now intensified to an almost unbearable degree, teased another growl from Eloise's stomach, making her smile as she finally headed for the bathroom. Obviously Bill knew his way around the kitchen and didn't mind doing the honors when it came to preparing their breakfast. And a little pampering always did a woman good, as he almost certainly had to know.

Her spirit of adventure—the same spirit of adventure that had prompted her to silently sing "let it snow" the previous evening—now firmly back in place, Eloise made short work of a hot shower. Anything could, and very likely would happen in the time she and Bill were together over the weekend. But deep in her heart she believed that all of it would also be good.

She dressed in the jeans she'd worn last night and a tailored white cotton shirt, applied a light touch of makeup and ran a brush through her hair, taming it easily into the pageboy style she favored. She took a few minutes more to make the bed and check the voice mail on her cell phone, and was relieved to find that no messages had been left for her.

Freed, at least for the time being, of any pressing con-

cerns, and thus feeling lighthearted, Eloise headed out
of her bedroom and down the hallway to the stairs. She
was tempted to look into Bill's bedroom, but forced herself to pass by the open doorway without stopping. If he
wanted her to see his bedroom he'd invite her into it.
Otherwise she thought it would probably be best to consider it off-limits.

As she came to the foot of the narrow flight of wooden
steps, Eloise paused for a long moment. She couldn't
help but delight in the bright and cheerful warmth of the
living area that made up the first floor of Bill's charming
cottage. Despite the gloomy prospect of gray sky hanging low outside the wall of windows, inside all appeared
to be wonderfully snug and cozy.

In the fireplace, flames licked merrily at the logs
stacked behind a mesh screen. Lamps glowed softly on
the end tables on either side of the cushy leather sofa.
And the small round wooden table in the dining alcove
was set with an eclectic mix of old-fashioned orange,
yellow and green pottery dishes.

The day might be dreary. But here in his lovely cottage Bill had made a place capable of soothing one's
soul no matter how nasty the weather outside happened
to be.

"I hope my rattling around in the kitchen didn't wake
you," he said. "Any pot banging on my part was purely
accidental."

He stood near the stove, a bright-yellow dish towel
casually tossed over one shoulder, a yellow pottery mug,
steam rising from it, held in his hand, a boyish grin on
his handsome face.

Dressed in faded jeans that had a vintage quality about
them and an equally faded black sweatshirt, sleeves
pushed up to his elbows, he looked much more casual,

not to mention much more approachable, than Eloise ever remembered him being. But then she hadn't been with him in anything other than a social, and thus more politically prominent setting, even seventeen years ago.

Here he didn't have to put on his public persona, and for that matter, neither did she. Here they really could be themselves without fear of repercussions from other outside entities.

Feeling just a little shy, as well as just a little excited—well, actually extremely excited—Eloise returned his smile as she crossed the living room and joined him in the kitchen.

"It was the luscious smell of coffee brewing and bacon frying that got me up," she admitted.

"I have fresh-squeezed orange juice, too, and eggs ready to scramble. I'm a breakfast eater, but I wasn't sure if you were, too."

"I am this morning," she assured him.

"Good." His grin widened appreciably. "Coffee first or juice?"

"Juice, and then coffee when the food's ready."

"Toast with your eggs and bacon?" he asked as he poured juice into a crystal glass, then handed it to her.

"Yes, please."

She sipped the juice, savoring its distinctive tang as he turned back to the stove and lit the gas flame under the skillet he had at the ready.

"You do like scrambled eggs, don't you?"

"My favorite," she admitted. "Can I do anything to help?"

"I think I have everything under control." He popped thick slices of whole-wheat bread into the double-slot toaster, poured the eggs into the heated skillet and checked on the bacon warming in the oven. "Help yourself to coffee whenever you're ready.'' He indicated a green mug just like his on the counter. ''There's sugar in the sugar bowl and cream in the refrigerator.''

''Thanks.''

''Do you take cream and sugar in your coffee?'' he asked, eyeing her curiously.

''Not unless it's so strong you can stand a spoon in it.''

''Mine's strong, but not that strong.'' He grinned at her again, then focused his attention on stirring the eggs in the skillet as he continued in a more serious tone. ''I'm just now realizing how much I don't know about you, Eloise. And that seems so odd because I feel as if I've known you forever.''

''I feel the same way,'' she said, surprised at how succinctly he'd stated her sentiments as well as his own. ''And it *is* weird to think that in a lot of ways we really are strangers.''

''I don't know about you, but I'm hoping maybe we can remedy the situation now that we finally have a little time alone together. There are so many things I want to know about you.''

''There are so many things I want to know about you, too.'' She set her empty juice glass in the sink, crossed to the counter to fill the green mug with coffee, then shot him a teasing glance. ''And I'd say we've already made a good start. I now know you can cook.''

''And I now know you take your coffee black and can be tempted to eat breakfast if scrambled eggs are on the menu.'' He smiled wryly as he spooned the eggs into a serving dish.

''Don't forget the whole-wheat toast,'' she added, retrieving the slices from the toaster as they popped up, then putting them on a bright orange plate to take to the table.

"Looks like everything's ready."

"Then let's eat."

They concentrated on their meal, intent on enjoying the food Bill had prepared while it was hot. They also traded bits and pieces of information about themselves. His favorite color was red and hers was green. Together, Bill quipped, they could easily end up looking a lot like Christmas unless they consulted on wardrobe choices before being seen with each other.

They also shared the same favorite travel destination outside the United States—anywhere in Italy, but especially Venice. That led Eloise to wonder aloud why they'd never run into each other there.

"Obviously bad timing on my part," Bill muttered ruefully.

"Or mine," Eloise said. "Although it's been several years since my last trip to Italy. Walter and I tried taking the boys to Venice when they were eight. They weren't really as interested in art museums and old churches as we thought they'd be, though. They did, however, think it would be great fun to jump off the bridges into the canals."

"Oh, no. They didn't, did they?" Bill asked, eyes wide with partially feigned horror.

"No, but not for lack of trying. One or the other of us was constantly hauling one or the other of them off a bridge railing the entire time we were in Venice."

"How about favorite travel destinations in the United States?"

"That's easy—San Francisco." Eloise smiled when he eyed her with surprise. "I'm a city girl, now. I love the hustle and bustle, nice hotels, good restaurants, museums, shopping.''

Bill laughed and shook his head.

''So there's no chance I'll ever be able to lure you to, say, the wilds of Montana?''

''Would I have to hike into the woods for miles and miles and then have to set up camp and cook over an open fire and sleep in a tent?''

''Only if you really wanted to. Otherwise you could stay at one of several lodges I can highly recommend, and enjoy all the comforts of home while I rough it with your sons for a few days.''

''I wonder if they'd enjoy doing something like that,'' Eloise mused, pushing her empty plate aside and sitting back in her chair, coffee mug in hand.

''Would you consider it if they showed some interest?''

''I most certainly would, but only as long as I could stay in one of your highly recommended lodges.''

''You have my word of honor on that. And, you know, Montana isn't all that far from San Francisco. We could always follow up the outdoor adventure with a little culture,'' Bill suggested.

''We most certainly could,'' Eloise agreed, her smile widening as she met his gaze across the table.

How easy it was to make plans with him, she thought. But then, unable to ignore her tendency toward the contrary where Bill Harper was concerned, she found herself wondering if their plans to take a trip together would end up being nothing more than a delightful fantasy.

Their lives would have to be intertwined on a much deeper level before they could ever really think about traveling together along with her sons. And right now they were merely friends, sharing a meal.

"Maybe by summer we'll be in a better position to consider a trip together more seriously," Bill said, seeming to read her sudden hesitation somewhere in her expression. "As for now the only real decision we have to make is whether to take a walk on the beach before or after I clean up the kitchen. I'll leave the choice up to you."

Standing, he began to gather their empty plates. Eloise stood, too, and followed him to the kitchen, carrying the serving dishes that had held their scrambled eggs, bacon and toast.

"How about after *we* clean up the kitchen?" she suggested. "Although I really should be the one to do it since you were kind enough to do all the cooking, and quite well, I might add."

"Thanks for the offer, but you're my guest here. I'm not letting you do KP duty alone. Any help you want to give will be greatly appreciated, however. And thanks, too, for complimenting my cooking abilities. I'm only hoping you'll feel the same after a few more meals.

"Lunch won't be too much of a challenge since there's sliced ham and turkey and cheese in the refrigerator for sandwiches. Deciding what to do with the salmon fillets I'd planned to fix for dinner might require more thought, though, especially since it's probably going to be too cold and too wet to fire up the grill on the deck outside. By the way, you do like salmon, don't you?"

"Oh, yes, but I usually poach mine in the oven. Sprinkled with herbs, a little lemon juice and some white wine and wrapped in foil, they're ready in thirty minutes or less."

"Sounds like an excellent alternative to me."

Bill finished loading the dishwasher, then crossed to a small pantry and opened the door.

"Lots of herbs and spices to choose from in here," he said, waving a hand at a rack that held at least two dozen glass jars, all neatly labeled. "There are fresh lemons in the refrigerator, along with a couple of bottles of white wine."

"Well then, we're all set."

Eloise folded the towel on which she'd been drying her hands and laid it over a rack, then smiled at Bill companionably. Amazing how comfortable she had been, bumping around the kitchen with him, helping with mundane domestic chores. They worked so well together, and their banter back and forth was so natural anyone looking in on them would have assumed they'd shared the same space for years instead of only a few hours.

She could be herself with him without suffering any qualms, and that seemed to be true of him, too. They not only liked each other, she realized, but to a great extent, they also trusted each other. And that trust provided a foundation of support upon which each of them could depend.

"We don't have to take a walk, you know," Bill said, his own smile suddenly, softly seductive. "We could curl up in front of the fire and be totally, completely lazy."

For just an instant Eloise was tempted. But a part of her wasn't quite ready yet to welcome the intimacy that would surely come with such languorous behavior. The closeness she felt toward Bill was still too new to act upon in a hasty manner.

She trusted him, but she also trusted her own instincts and inclinations. And just then she thought a little fresh air along with some hearty exercise would do them both good.

"Why don't we take a walk while we can?" she suggested. "It might rain again later."

"You're probably right. But be sure to bundle up. I don't want you catching a chill out there."

"Be right back, then."

Upstairs in her bedroom, Eloise took Bill's advice to heart, pulling on a heavy, fisherman-knit sweater before donning her jacket. She dug out the wool hat that she'd packed in her overnight bag and added it to the gloves and scarf she had at the ready, then headed downstairs again.

Bill stood by the French doors, also dressed for the cold, damp weather in a bulky black leather bomber jacket, a rakish red wool hat and matching scarf, and black leather gloves. As they stepped out on the deck, the icy air stole away Eloise's breath, sending a tiny shiver down her spine.

"Still game?" he asked, shooting a wry glance her way.

"I admit it's colder than I expected, but it's not raining and the wind isn't blowing too hard. Once we start walking, I'm sure we'll warm up."

"More than likely," he agreed.

Taking her gloved hand in his, he led her down the wooden steps that would take them down to the walkway across the dunes.

Considering the dreariness of the day, Eloise's spirits lightened even more as they set out together along the beach just out of reach of the lapping waves. The water was surprisingly calm, as was the wind that blew in occasional gentle gusts, lifting and twirling the ends of their scarves. Beneath their boots, the wet sand, packed firm, provided safe footing, crunching rhythmically as they walked. And while the air tasted of more rain to come, for the time being, at least, the promise seemed a distant one.

Conversation didn't seem all that necessary for the time being, either. Eloise would have been happy to talk if Bill had made the effort to initiate a discussion of any sort. But he appeared to be in a reflective mood, and seemed to be as content as she with the tranquil silence that stretched comfortably between them.

Only twice did they pass other walkers on the deserted beach—an older couple with a mannerly golden retriever and two young women with three energetic toddlers between them. Muffled as they all were in coats, hats and scarves, they were equally unrecognizable, the greetings they exchanged carried away in the wind along with the cries of the gulls circling overhead.

At some point along the way, Bill let go of Eloise's hand and put his arm around her shoulders. She gladly drew close to the shelter his body offered, and with a sense of homecoming, she slipped her arm around his waist, as well.

She wasn't sure how long or how far they'd walked when he finally suggested they return to the house. Invigorated and warmed by the physical and emotional closeness they shared, she felt as if she could walk with him forever. Wisely, however, Bill had apparently realized that eventually she would start to tire, as she had by the time his cottage finally came into view again.

"Ready to go in?" he asked, pausing by the walkway across the dunes. "Or would you like to walk awhile longer in another direction?"

"I'm definitely ready to go in," she admitted. "How about you?"

"Yes, I'm ready, too."

As if to confirm that they'd made the right decision, a light drizzle started to fall.

"Talk about perfect timing," Eloise said, laughing as they hurried up the steps and across the deck. "If we had walked even a little farther, we would have gotten soaked."

"We did hit it lucky, didn't we?"

Bill grinned at her as he slipped his key into the door lock, and Eloise grinned back at him. Then time suddenly seemed to stand still, the moment stretching out infinitely as their gazes locked.

Slowly, almost tentatively, Bill touched a gloved hand to Eloise's cheek. His smile faded, replaced by a questioning look to which her heart answered *Yes…yes, please….*

Wordlessly he bent his head and claimed her mouth with a chaste and gentle kiss, his lips first cold, then oh, so warm against her own. She raised up on tiptoe, eager to get closer to him, and with a low groan he deepened their kiss, but only for an instant.

Surprised by his sudden withdrawal, Eloise blinked up at him in confusion.

"Come inside," he said, his voice low. "Come inside where we can truly be alone together."

Chapter Nine

Bill knew he should have expected Eloise to distance herself from him once they were inside the cottage again. She had been doing exactly that—following a pattern, mostly in small ways—since the night he'd taken her to the Mayor's Ball.

She seemed to want to develop a closer relationship with him. Yet each time he made a move in that direction, she would allow him to go only so far. Then she would retreat behind a facade of sorts, using a polite tone and pretty manners to put him off.

But Bill had thought he'd finally breached the most steadfast of her ramparts when he kissed her on the deck outside the cottage door. She had seemed so relaxed and happy on their long, languorous walk. And she had met his gaze so openly as he'd paused to slide the key into the door lock.

He had been sure, from the look in her eyes, that she

had finally begun to trust him. And he had hoped that she understood he would never betray her trust in any way.

He had meant, more than anything, to reassure her of his regard with his kiss. And her obvious disappointment when he'd broken away to get them into the house again, and out of public view, had made him think that he'd succeeded.

But in the moments it had taken him to close and lock the French doors and turn to her once more, she had scurried across the living room, shedding hat, scarf, gloves and, almost reluctantly, her jacket before halting in front of the fireplace.

Holding her outdoor clothing folded over one arm, she turned her back on him and stretched out her free hand to the still faintly flickering flames of the fire he'd laid earlier.

Puzzled by the mixed signals she seemed to be giving, and admittedly even a little annoyed, Bill stuffed his hat, scarf and gloves into his jacket pockets and hung the jacket itself on the coatrack just inside the entryway. Keeping his distance, as she apparently wanted him to do, he stood for several moments, hands on his hips, and tried to decide what to say to her.

Perhaps, he concluded after a last moment's hesitation, he'd be wise to get his most pressing concern out in the open. He had never been one to play games when another person's feelings were involved. By the same token, he didn't want anyone, especially Eloise, playing games with him, either.

"Are you afraid of me?" he asked, unable to hide the very real distress such a possibility had begun to cause him.

Startled, Eloise turned to meet his gaze, the expression on her lovely face one of utter chagrin.

"Oh, Bill, no...I'm not...not at all." She took a step toward him, then stopped, confusion warring with her continued dismay. "Why would you think that?"

"Because you don't always seem completely comfortable with me. Like just now. You not only let me kiss you out on the deck, you also kissed me back. But then, as soon as we walked into the house, you couldn't seem to get away from me fast enough. You do know that I would never force myself on you, don't you? I'd never hurt you in any way if I could help it. You mean too much to me for that to ever happen."

"I know that, Bill, really I do. You've always behaved like a perfect gentleman when we're together, and I trust that you always will. Otherwise I would never have come here with you in the first place."

"Have I been out of line kissing you, then?" he prodded, really wanting to know, needing to know. Then he added before she could respond, just to reassure her yet again, "Because I won't do it again if you feel I have. Although I admit it won't be easy. You're so damned kissable sometimes, it may, on occasion, be almost impossible for me to resist. But I will, if that's what you want."

He paused in his recitation, then smiled ruefully, aware that he'd embarrassed her when a blush suffused her face, tinting her cheeks a pretty shade of pink.

"You haven't been the least bit out of line." She smiled, too, with a wry twist to her lips. "As you pointed out so kindly, I *have* been kissing you back. And it's been very nice...kissing you...."

"But?" he prompted, aware that she still had reservations and wanting to know why.

"But I'm not sure it's a good idea for us to get…involved, at least not too…deeply, under the circumstances." She paused, a pained expression on her face as she looked away.

"You're not involved in a relationship with another man, are you?

"Oh, no, not at all." She met his gaze again, unable to hide her bewilderment.

"And I'm not involved with another woman. So basically we're both free to be together if we want, aren't we?"

"Yes," she agreed, her confusion still much in evidence.

"And I'm assuming you want to be here with me today. Is that right, too?" he asked, encouraging her with a soft smile.

"Yes…"

"Good." He nodded once in affirmation, then added, "I want to be here with you today, too."

Still meeting his gaze, she smiled again, though tentatively.

"We're also comfortable together, aren't we?" he continued.

"Yes…"

"And if I happen to make you feel uncomfortable in any way, I want you to tell me, all right?"

"Yes, of course."

"No more pulling away without an explanation?"

"No," she replied in a thoroughly repentant tone. "No more pulling away without an explanation."

"Because it's not much fun for me always having to worry that I've said or done something wrong, but at the same time never knowing for sure what, if anything, it might have been."

"Sounds like I've been a bit of a brat," Eloise conceded. Still meeting his gaze, she smiled again, more than a hint of mischievous pride now in evidence.

"Yes, you most certainly have." Experiencing an almost palpable sense of relief, Bill met her smile with one of his own.

He knew now how it must feel to traverse a minefield without being blown to bits and pieces. He could have so easily chosen all the wrong words and deepened the divide that had begun to yawn between them. Instead he'd found a way to help Eloise set aside the lingering anxiety she'd been feeling on her own there with him.

"I promise I'll do better from now on," she said.

"That's all I'm asking." He quirked an eyebrow at her inquiringly. "Now how about letting me help you hang up your jacket so you can relax and stay awhile."

"I think I can manage that task on my own," she assured him, crossing to the coatrack.

"Independent little lady, aren't you?" He allowed his grin to take on a teasing cast.

"I take exception to *little,* but otherwise, yes I am, and don't you forget it."

The look she shot his way had enough steel underlying the amusement in it to assure him she'd meant what she'd said.

"Believe me, I won't," he murmured with the solemnity of a vow taken. Then he turned away and headed for the kitchen. "Hungry?"

"Mmm, I hate to admit it after eating such a big breakfast, but yes, very hungry."

"Blame it on the long walk we took out in the fresh air. That's what I'm doing," he advised as he opened the refrigerator door, grabbed the packages of deli ham, smoked turkey and cheese, and set them on the counter.

Together they fixed towering sandwiches on slabs of whole-wheat bread, adding mustard, lettuce and tomato to the meats and cheese. At Bill's instruction, Eloise looked for and found a bag of corn chips in the pantry while he opened a bottle of white wine and filled a glass for each of them. He then suggested they eat on the sofa in front of the fire instead of at the table in the dining alcove, and Eloise readily agreed.

While she ferried plates and glasses and wine bottle to the small coffee table, he added more kindling to the glowing coals remaining in the firebox. Soon flames were licking up again, warming them across the hearth.

"It's a shame you can't spend more time here," Eloise said after munching contentedly on her sandwich for a few minutes. "I can't remember feeling quite this relaxed in a long time."

"I know what you mean," Bill replied. "I've thought of escaping here more often, but then I imagine what it would be like if the press found out about my secret hideaway. Somehow I don't think it would be very relaxing at all if there were media vans parked in the driveway."

"Point taken." Eloise glanced at him, the inquiring look in her eyes underscoring her next words. "Of course, you could have more of a private, personal life once you've reached the term limit for mayor of New York City. Unless you decide to run for another political office, of course—governor of the state, maybe, or United States senator."

"That's assuming I can win the next mayoral election," he pointed out pragmatically. "There's always a chance I'm already in my *last* term as mayor even as we speak."

"Only if you chose not to run again."

"I appreciate the vote of confidence." He smiled as he reached for his wineglass.

"Only one of many, I assure you." She hesitated a moment, then added, "Are you going to run for mayor again?"

Bill considered Eloise's question as he looked into the fire. So many times over the past couple of years the responsibilities he'd taken on as mayor of one of the world's largest cities had seemed almost overwhelming. Having to rebuild New York and revitalize its citizens after the havoc wreaked by terrorists had been a formidable undertaking.

But the recovery was already progressing well, and he wanted to see it through to a successful completion. And that would require another term in office.

"Barring any unforeseen difficulties, yes, I'm going to run for mayor again," he acknowledged at last, looking over at Eloise as he spoke.

She met his gaze, the expression on her face one he couldn't quite read. Then she focused her attention on the flames leaping merrily in the fireplace as she continued in a lighthearted tone that didn't quite ring true.

"And then on to the governor's mansion or the United States Senate, and eventually the White House?"

"That would depend on several variables I haven't fully taken into consideration just yet. A lot will depend on what's happening in my life a few years from now. We both know how impossible it is to predict the future. I'm not ruling anything out, but I admit that I've been thinking more and more lately about how nice it would be to lead a more personal, less political life."

Reaching out, Bill took Eloise's empty plate from her and set it on the coffee table. He refilled both of their wineglasses, then sat back again and took her hand in his. "But what would you do if you got out of politics altogether?" she asked, twining her fingers through his companionably.

"Practice law, maybe, or teach at a college or university, maybe even run a nonprofit organization," he replied, his tone suddenly teasing.

"Which is not as easy as you might think in New York City, especially lately," Eloise retorted. "As you well know. Although I'd be happy to explain in detail the current obstacles—"

"But sadly, can't since we called a time-out on that particular subject for the duration of the weekend," he cut in hastily, determined not to let his imprudent attempt at humor spoil the day.

"And lucky for you, too."

"Very lucky," he agreed, giving her hand a squeeze that, to his relief, she returned with equal fervor. "I'd also have more time to spend here."

"But you might get bored."

"Not with the right person keeping me company, as well as keeping me on my toes. Care to apply for the position?"

Though Bill made sure his tone wasn't the least bit serious, and he grinned as he asked the question, he all but held his breath, waiting for Eloise to reply.

Her eyes alight with mischief, she played the moment for all it was worth, twirling her wineglass as she contemplated its contents. Finally, with a hint of playfulness he assumed was meant to match his own, she glanced at him.

"I might," she answered. "Depending on the circumstances, of course."

"Of course."

Not a definite, count-upon yes, but not a refusal to

even consider the idea, either, he consoled himself as he gathered their plates, stood and carried them to the kitchen.

"There are brownies left over from last night and fresh strawberries in the refrigerator," he offered. "I saw a carton of Dutch chocolate ice cream in the freezer, too, if you're in the mood for some dessert? I could always open another bottle of wine, too."

"More wine sounds nice," Eloise said as she bent over to untie the laces on her boots.

"More wine it is, then."

He replaced the empty bottle with a full one, then moved to the antique wardrobe standing against the wall on one side of the fireplace. Opening the doors, he revealed a CD player and a small television set. He popped a CD into the player and pushed the play button. The first chords of a piano piece, soft and mellow, drifted from the speakers.

"Do you like George Winston?" he asked as he joined Eloise on the sofa again.

"I like him if he's the one playing on your CD." She slipped off her boots, wriggled her toes in her woolly socks, then propped her feet on the coffee table. "The music suits the day."

"I think so, too."

Bill, too, unlaced his boots and took them off, then stretched out his legs and propped his feet on the coffee table, as well.

"Mmm, it sounds like it's raining again."

"Nice, isn't it, listening to it tap against the windows from such a warm and cozy vantage?"

"Very nice."

She looked over at him, her pale-gray eyes sleepy, and Bill thought about kissing her. But he held back when the corners of her mouth turned down in the tiniest of frowns.

"Something wrong?" he asked, unable to hide his sudden concern.

"I was just wondering…"

"What?"

"It's really none of my business." She shrugged her shoulders with seeming diffidence as she slid her gaze away again.

"If it's something to do with me and it's worrying you in some way, then I wish you'd tell me. I don't want you upsetting yourself when it might not be necessary."

"Okay, then, I was just wondering if you spent much time here with…Marnie," she said after hesitating indecisively a few moments more.

"Marnie?" he repeated, slightly taken aback by Eloise's unexpected mention of his ex-wife's name.

His ten-year marriage to Marnie Hartwell was a subject he rarely, if ever, discussed with anyone. He hadn't considered it a matter with which Eloise would concern herself, especially since the marriage had ended amicably almost seven years ago.

Once his initial surprise, not to mention consternation, had faded, however, Bill could understand her interest. He had brought her to the very private place he'd come to consider his home. And though he had done so teasingly, he'd let her know that he hoped they would be able to spend time there together in the future.

It was only natural that she'd want to be sure certain ghosts had been laid to rest before she committed to a more serious relationship with him. The same had been true of Marnie.

Only, he had never been able to convince his ex-wife

that he no longer had feelings for Eloise Vale because he always had and he'd known he always would. Eventually, unable to accept that her husband could never love her as completely as she had every right to expect, Marnie had divorced him. Then she had gone on to find the happiness she deserved with someone else, and Bill had been glad for her.

"I knew it would be a mistake to ask about her," Eloise muttered, setting her wineglass on the coffee table and folding her arms across her chest defensively.

"It wasn't a mistake at all," he chided her quietly as he slipped an arm around her shoulders. "You just caught me by surprise, and there's nothing wrong with that, either. Like I said, it's nice having someone around who can keep me on my toes.

"And, to answer your question, Marnie only came here a few times. The house was in pretty bad shape then. It was too much like camping out for her taste, as I'm sure you can appreciate.

"I wanted to work on the remodeling myself so I wouldn't let her hire a contractor to get the job done. Looking back, I realize now that I used this place as a getaway in more ways than one, and I didn't try very hard to make a secret of it where Marnie was concerned."

"But if you loved her enough to marry her, why would you want to spend time away from her?"

Though Eloise had leaned against him at his urging, she'd done so with seeming reluctance. But there was no challenge in her voice as she questioned him, only a hint of bemusement.

Bill wondered what she'd heard about his marriage and eventual divorce. Likely very little because Marnie had made an effort to stay out of the limelight as much as possible. And when they'd split up, they had done so without any real acrimony or any overt publicity. By the time he'd run for mayor, his bachelor status was well established and accepted, and his former marriage such old news that it was of no interest to anyone.

Now, however, he didn't mind answering whatever questions Eloise had. He wanted more than anything to reassure her that while he had loved Marnie in a way, and she would always have a place in his heart, she had never been the love of his life.

"I thought I did at the time. I met her when I was at a very real low point in my life. You had turned down my proposal and proceeded with your plans to marry Walter. I wasn't feeling too good about myself and as a result I'd become a bit of a recluse. Some friends of mine decided an intervention was in order. They dragged me to a party, and Marnie was there with some of her friends.

"She was at loose ends, too, feeling lonely after ending a relationship, and one thing led to another. We seemed to have enough in common to make a marriage work. We enjoyed each other's company and we had the same values. She was also just as involved with furthering her publishing career as I was with achieving my political aspirations. Our work kept us apart a lot of the time, but we had fun when we were together.

"Eventually, though, Marnie wanted more than a high-power job, an apartment in the city and a social life that revolved around my climb up the political ladder. She wanted to quit her job, buy a house in the suburbs and raise babies. I kept putting her off, saying the time wasn't right.

"She finally realized that if the time wasn't right after almost ten years of marriage, it would never be right.

When she said as much to me, I agreed. We had drifted so far apart by then, and the fondness we still managed to feel for each other was so close to disappearing altogether that we decided it would be best to file for divorce.''

''Are you sorry now that you didn't try harder to make your marriage work? Maybe if you'd had a child...'' Eloise glanced at him, a sad look in her eyes.

''I wish I could say it would have been that easy. But having a child wouldn't have solved our problems. It would have only added more problems, and it would have made our parting, inevitable as it was, that much more painful to bear.

''In all honesty, I didn't love Marnie the way she deserved to be loved, and somewhere in the back of my mind, I knew it from the very beginning. I couldn't, in good conscience, father a child when my marriage had already become a burden I no longer wanted to carry.''

''I'm so sorry, Bill,'' Eloise murmured. ''Sorry you didn't find the kind of happiness with Marnie that *you* deserved.''

''I'm sorry, too, but I only had myself to blame. If I'd paid more attention to my heart than my head, I would have realized what a mistake I was making before I'd actually made it. But marrying Marnie looked good on paper, so to speak. And I didn't think I'd have anything to lose because I'd already lost you.

''I never once considered what Marnie had to lose, and I'll always regret that. I'm just glad that I not only eventually came to my senses, but that Marnie now has a wonderful husband who adores her, a lovely house in Connecticut and two bright, beautiful children she can dote on with a third one on the way.''

''Do you still keep in touch with her?''

"Not on a regular basis. We have mutual friends, so occasionally we attend the same parties, and we still exchange cards at Christmas."

Eloise uttered a soft sigh and tipped her head against his shoulder. But Bill still sensed a thread of tension running through her, making him wonder if he'd said more about his marriage to Marnie than he should have. He'd only wanted to be truthful with Eloise so that she would trust him. Maybe he'd been too truthful, though—if that was possible.

"I thought when you married Marnie that you must not have really cared that much about me, after all," she said after several moments of silence had stretched between them. "I thought you'd just moved on quite happily after I chose to honor my engagement to Walter."

"I didn't really have any choice *but* to move on," he pointed out as kindly as he could. "You made your feelings very clear, or maybe I should say your lack of feelings for me. Although I could have sworn at the time that you were as much in love with me as I was with you.

"But then, the night I proposed to you, you walked away from me without a backward glance, and I told myself I must have only imagined the sexual tension between us. All we'd ever really done was exchange a few passionate kisses—very passionate kisses, but only kisses, after all.

"I couldn't really believe I'd been so wrong about you, though. In fact, I've never believed the sparks that flew between us when we were together were merely a figment of my imagination.

"I admit that I had moments when I doubted myself seventeen years ago, but somewhere deep inside me I knew that we belonged together. The way you've kissed me the past week has made me even more certain that I was right about us. Which has had me wondering…''

''What?'' she asked, looking at him, her eyes wide and inquiring.

''First question—why wouldn't you admit to your feelings for me then? Second question—can you finally acknowledge how you feel about me now? I've been honest with you, Eloise. I've answered all the questions you've asked. I think you owe me some answers and some honesty in return.''

Chapter Ten

Eloise stared wordlessly at the flickering fire as she plucked with nervous fingers at the fabric of her jeans. How neatly Bill had backed her into a corner, she thought, and a truly uncomfortable corner at that. But in all honesty—the honesty he expected of her—she had only herself to blame for the tack their conversation had taken.

She had been the one to bring up Bill's personal life. And as he'd said, he had answered her questions in a forthright manner. Lulled by her sense of companionship with him, heightened no doubt by the wine she'd drunk, she had brought out into the open certain concerns that she would have normally kept to herself.

That he now assumed she would be equally honest with him was easily understandable. But forming the replies he wanted required the kind of soul-searching she would just as soon have avoided.

So many times over the past seventeen years Eloise had thought of Bill, not only with longing, but also with regret. But she had schooled herself religiously to block out those memories and the emotions they inevitably stirred deep inside her.

She had believed that her first loyalty belonged to the man she'd chosen to marry. And she had done her best to honor the commitment she'd made to Walter Vale in her thoughts as well as in her deeds.

Not that being a good, loving and faithful wife to Walter had been difficult for her—not at all. Her affection for her husband had been deep and abiding. Much as Marnie had with Bill, Walter had come into her life at a low point.

Following the unexpected deaths of first her mother, then only a few months later, her father, she had been feeling as if she'd been cast adrift in a very lonely world. Older than she by almost twenty years, Walter had filled a very painful gap.

He had treated her with kindness, and he had shown her admiration and respect. He had made her laugh again, and he had given her hope for the future. With him, Eloise had felt deeply cherished, and for him, she had felt not only tenderness, but gratitude, as well.

Walter's kisses might not have stirred the same intensity of passion within her as Bill Harper's had. But she had known that passion alone could be all too fleeting. And Bill's true passion seventeen years ago had been attaining political success.

Walter, by comparison, already had a successful career as an investment banker, and he was eager to devote his time and attention to a wife and family. And back then Eloise had thought she needed that time and attention more than anything.

She had made her choices accordingly. And out of respect for Walter, she had refused to allow herself to consider any alternate might-have-been, especially where Bill Harper had been concerned. As a result she'd enjoyed a relatively happy marriage, and with the birth of her sons she'd had the family she had always wanted. Eventually, too, with the creation of Manhattan Multiples, she'd also had a satisfying and productive career of her own.

She couldn't apologize—*wouldn't* apologize—to Bill for the decision she'd made. But she could explain it to him and hope he would understand that she had never meant to hurt him. In all honesty, she hadn't thought she could.

Gently, Bill placed a calming hand over her anxious fingers, stilling their repetitive motion. Brought back to the present moment, Eloise looked up and met his unrelenting gaze.

"Is it so hard for you to talk to me?" he asked in a quiet voice.

"I was just remembering the past, trying to sort out my thoughts so I could be as honest with you as you've asked me to be."

"And?" he urged even more quietly, giving her hand a reassuring squeeze.

"Regarding your first question, I didn't want to admit to my feelings for you seventeen years ago. Not because they weren't real. Sparks did fly between us those times we were together. And when you kissed me it seemed like my whole world was suddenly spinning out of control...*my* control.

"I seemed to lose myself in you and that frightened me. You could so easily have become the center of my universe. But I didn't believe at the time that I would ever be that important to you.

"You were just starting out in politics, full of plans to save the world and other great places. You had people to meet and places to go. We had only just met, and yes, our emotions were extremely intense at the time. But I couldn't imagine how that degree of fervor could last. I didn't think you were ready to take on the responsibility of a wife, much less the family I wanted. And I couldn't help but wonder what would happen to us once our infatuation for each other wore off.

"There was also the fact that I was engaged to Walter, and I loved him, too. Although I admit my feelings for him weren't as madly passionate as my feelings for you, it seemed to me that my relationship with him was much more apt to stand the test of time.

"I never realized until today how deeply you were affected when I turned down your proposal, and for that I'm truly sorry. I misjudged you in that way, at least. As to whether a marriage between us would have lasted…" Eloise shrugged her shoulders and uttered a soft sigh. "I guess that's one thing we'll never know."

"No, we won't," Bill agreed, his voice tinged with sadness.

"Please don't think that I blithely walked away from you without any regrets, though," she continued determinedly, glancing up at him. "Turning down your proposal was one of the most difficult things I've ever had to do. But once I'd made my decision I couldn't allow myself to look back. Walter deserved to have my loyalty as well as my love, and during all the years we were married he never gave me a reason to believe otherwise."

"I wish I could say I'd have been a better husband to

you than I was to Marnie. I'd like to believe that I would have been,'' Bill said, threading his fingers through hers. ''But truth be told, my political aspirations *were* first and foremost in my life back then. I knew I had a limited amount of time to build support, and I wasn't willing to let much of anything get in my way.

''At the time, all I really wanted was to have you with me as I followed my dreams. Looking back, I have to admit that I didn't really take your dreams into consideration. I just assumed you'd automatically match them to my own.''

''Typical man.'' She couldn't help but tease him. ''Thanks for being so honest, though.''

''Hey, I'm not saying your wants and needs would have been completely unimportant to me,'' he protested. ''You meant so much to me. I would never have done anything intentionally to upset you.''

''I know.'' Eloise took a turn at giving his hand a reassuring squeeze.

''But I *was* just a little self-centered seventeen years ago, and please note my emphasis on *was*.''

''I'll do that,'' she replied with a wry smile.

''Because that was then, and this is now. And you've only answered my first question.'' Bending his head, Bill feathered a light trail of kisses from Eloise's temple along her cheek to the corner of her mouth. ''The second question being—in case you've forgotten—can you finally acknowledge how you feel about me now?''

The warm, tender, coaxing touch of his lips against her sensitive skin sent a rush of heated longing zinging through her. She wanted to turn to him, to put her arms around him, to pull him closer for a deeper, more complete kiss—exactly the kind of kiss they'd shared several times already.

Yet she hesitated, holding back, aware that alone with him here such a kiss would likely be a prelude to something much more intense and much more intimate. And she wasn't sure she was ready for that intensity or that ultimate intimacy meant to bond a man and woman as nothing else could.

Bill had admitted that seventeen years ago he'd assumed her dreams would match his own. He had also made sure she understood that attitude was an old and long-discarded one.

But he might now assume that if she lowered her defenses with him on a physical and emotional level, she'd be more understanding of—and thus more amenable to—his stand on certain not-to-be-mentioned issues on which they currently held differing opinions. And on which they would continue to hold differing opinions long after these fleeting weekend moments had passed.

"Not a good sign," Bill prompted lightly, making her glance up at him uncomfortably.

"Why do you say that?" she asked, knowing the answer but wanting to buy just a little more time.

"I was hoping for a spontaneous, not to mention positive response. Something on the order of 'yes, yes, I love you madly.' But you're obviously having to give it quite a bit of thought, and I have to admit that doesn't exactly bode well for me."

"I wish it were that simple," Eloise acknowledged, holding his gaze. "If we were an ordinary couple with only minor responsibilities to other people…" She shrugged helplessly, hopelessly as her words trailed away. Then she added in a definitive tone, "But we're not."

"What about our responsibility to ourselves and to each other, and our right to finally have the happiness we deserve?'' he insisted. ''How much good are we going to be to other people if we can't be good to ourselves and each other first?

''Although maybe I'm assuming too much here. Maybe this time I *am* the only one feeling sparks fly when we kiss. And to my way of thinking, that's pretty simple. So if it's true, just say so before I really make a fool of myself.''

Letting go of her hand and withdrawing his arm from around her shoulders, Bill moved away from her on the sofa, then turned so that he faced her fully. He didn't appear angry or upset. He merely seemed resigned to receiving her rebuff as he steadily held her gaze.

He couldn't have made it any easier for her to call the shots if he'd tried. All she had to do was tell him he'd misread her signals, and that would be the end of that. Yet it wasn't easy at all because he'd asked her to be honest, too.

Telling him she'd felt nothing special when they'd kissed would be the worst kind of lie because it would make him doubt himself when he hadn't any reason to.

And he was right about their responsibility to themselves and each other. They did deserve a little happiness, and there was no one with whom she wanted to share that happiness more than Bill Harper.

''Sometimes I can be such a ninny.'' Reaching out, she gently cupped his face with both of her hands, then leaned forward and oh-so-tentatively kissed him on the lips. ''Of course I feel sparks fly when we kiss. I feel sparks fly when you walk into a room and your gaze locks with mine. I feel sparks fly when you shoot a smile my way and when we share a good laugh and even when you glare at me as you argue a point. Right here, right now, I'm crazy about you, Bill Harper. And I apologize for letting you believe, even for a moment, that I wasn't.''

Slowly as she spoke, his expression changed. His resignation faded and his eyes widened with surprise. Finally he smiled with undisguised delight, filling Eloise with an overwhelming sense of relief. Her hedging had almost spoiled everything, but her sincerity—a sincerity coming straight from her heart—had ultimately saved the day.

''Apology accepted,'' Bill said, his voice soft and deep. Putting his arms around her, he drew her into his embrace. She went willing, resting her hands on his chest as she smiled up at him. ''Now let's kiss and make up.''

''Oh, yes, let's do that,'' she agreed, welcoming the masterful claiming of his mouth on hers without the slightest hint of hesitation.

The self-imposed need to hold back what she'd clung to for so long disappeared. She was a grown woman with valid wants and needs, and she wanted, *needed* Bill Harper in a way she was only now able to acknowledge. The restraints she'd imposed upon herself fell away because they were no longer necessary, and she kissed him back with an urgency that spoke of true emotions too long denied.

As if sensing the removal of all former boundaries between them, Bill moved his hands over Eloise's body as their kiss deepened even more. He seemed to want to touch every part of her—his fingers stroking her back, then traveling down to graze the swell of her breasts before pausing at her waist, then finally splaying over her hips possessively.

She, too, savored the opportunity for more tactile contact, rubbing her palms against the sweatshirt covering his chest, then down, as well, until her hands came to the leather belt cinching his jeans. Without really thinking, she tugged at it, subconsciously willing it away so that she could free the T-shirt he also wore and slide her hands against his bare skin.

Raising his head, Bill broke off their kiss, causing her to murmur a protest as she looked up at him. He smiled reassuringly and smoothed a hand over her hair.

"I was just thinking…" he began, then paused long enough to give her a hard, quick kiss, as if he couldn't help himself.

"About what?" she asked in a dreamy voice.

"About the possibility that we'd be much more comfortable upstairs…in my bedroom…in my bed," he answered, interspersing his words with more quick little kisses. "But I don't want to rush you."

Eloise couldn't help but giggle as she said, "Not really much of a rush since we've already waited seventeen years."

"Yeah, well, my sentiments exactly, but I wasn't sure how you'd feel about it."

"Like I said, I'm crazy about you, Bill Harper, and I don't intend to pretend I'm not, even for a moment."

"I'm crazy about you, too, Eloise Vale. And I can't think of anything I want to do more than show you just how much you mean to me." He stood, pulling her with him all in one fluid motion. "Let me make love to you— long, slow, sweet love…"

"Oh, yes, please…"

Together, hand in hand, they walked up the narrow wooden staircase. The CD had long since stopped playing, and the only sound that broke the silence was the steady, continuous beat of rain against the windows.

With the onset of late afternoon the stormy sky had

turned an even deeper shade of gray. Without any lights lit upstairs, Bill's bedroom seemed as dark as a hidden cave, but still, to Eloise, infinitely welcoming.

Letting go of her hand, Bill crossed to a tall chest on the far wall and turned on the small, silk-shaded lamp that sat on it. The low-wattage bulb cast just enough glow to bring the rest of the room's furnishings—old-fashioned mahogany sleigh-bed, single nightstand, three-drawer dresser and an upholstered chair—into relief.

Eloise also saw the little stone fireplace, laid ready with fresh kindling and stacked logs.

"What a lovely bedroom," she said, following after Bill as he moved to the hearth and took a box of matches from the mantel.

"I have to agree, but it's even lovelier having you here to share it with me," he replied, smiling at her as he knelt and struck the match.

He had the fire crackling warmly in a matter of minutes with only a minimum of poking and prodding. Then he stood again and drew her close, just holding her for several moments in an embrace that made her feel truly cherished.

"I can't tell you how many times I've thought of being here with you just like this," he said at last, looking into her eyes, his own gaze intense, open and inviting.

"I've thought about being with you, too, although I never pictured us together in a place quite as perfect as this," she admitted, rubbing her cheek against his chest.

"So you had visions of us in a clinch atop my desk at city hall?" he teased.

"Actually I've always had a thing for elevators," she retorted, giving his arm a gentle, playful punch.

"I'll have to keep that in mind for another time, but right now, all kidding aside...." He swept her slight body into his arms, strode the short distance to his bed and tumbled her carefully onto the green and blue block quilt covering it. "This is exactly where I want you and mean to have you. Unless you're having second thoughts…"

"Not a chance of that happening," she answered him, opening her arms to him as he lay down beside her. "I'm right where I want to be, here with you."

Bill looked deep into her eyes for an instant longer, as if to assure himself that she spoke the truth. And then, with a low growl of satisfaction at what he had to have seen in her gaze, he pulled her into his arms and proceeded to kiss her nearly senseless.

He took his time, of course, tasting her slowly, then inviting her to taste him in return. He balanced long, slow, deep kisses with nibbling kisses that teased sighs from her as he alternately attended to the curve of her neck, the line of her jaw and the tender skin of her earlobes.

He soon had her plucking at the fabric of his clothing, until as last she'd unfastened his belt buckle and freed his T-shirt from the waistband of his jeans. She rubbed her hands over his hot, bare skin, first up along his muscular chest, then down across his abdomen, at which point he caught her wrists and rolled her onto her back.

Smiling up at him, she grabbed the hem of his sweatshirt and tugged on it insistently.

"Take it off…please…."

"Not yet."

He grabbed her wrists again and held them in one hand. Then he tugged her shirt free and slipped his hand under it until he cupped one of her breasts possessively in his palm.

"Hey, no fair," she murmured, though she arched delicately into his caress. "I want to touch you, too."

"But I want to watch you as I touch you, and I'd be too distracted if I let you put your hands on me at the same time."

As if to emphasize his point, he rubbed his thumb over her nipple, causing her to tip her head back and moan softly.

"You are so beautiful and so damned responsive," he muttered, moving his hand down her body, then deftly unzipping her jeans.

Knowing what he intended to do next, Eloise lifted her hips invitingly and was immediately rewarded when he slid his fingers down her belly until they barely, temptingly grazed her womanhood.

Bill moved his hand away with a masculine chuckle, then released his hold on her wrists.

"How about you take off all your clothes?" he suggested, nibbling a kiss on her neck.

"How about you take off all your clothes, too?" she suggested in return, lifting an inquiring eyebrow in such a way that he chuckled again.

"Okay, it's a deal."

He swung off the bed and pulled his sweatshirt and T-shirt over his head in one single, swift motion. Eloise sat up, her gaze fixed on his bare chest, still lightly bronzed with the last of his summer tan.

"What?" he asked smiling slightly.

"Just...you...seeing you like this...it's giving me goosebumps."

"Come here," he ordered.

Reaching out, he pulled her across the bed. She knelt up in front of him and put her arms around him, basking in the feel of his naked skin against her hands and face as he hugged her close. "Now," he continued, grabbing the hem of her sweater. "Let's get rid of this." He pulled it over her head. "And this…" He unbuttoned her blouse with amazing dexterity. "And, of course, this, too." He slid a finger under one strap of her lacy bra.

"Okay, okay." She giggled, feeling suddenly young and sexy and so desirable.

With much additional laughing and teasing, or perhaps in spite of it, Eloise thought, they managed to discard the remainder of their clothing. Then, suddenly much more solemn, Bill drew back the covers and Eloise snuggled into his bed. From the drawer in the nightstand, he took out a box of condoms, but though he was obviously ready physically, he set them aside for the time being.

"You make me feel like a teenager," he said as he lay down beside her and gathered her into his arms again.

"I know what you mean. Being here with you, making love like this, laughing together, I feel so young and carefree. I'm so glad I decided to follow my heart."

"So am I."

Starting all over again, Bill kissed Eloise on the mouth, then gradually worked his way down her body. He paid special attention to her breasts, teasing her nipples with gentle teeth and soothing tongue. He nibbled at her belly button, hands on her slim hips, and then had her writhing, nearly out of control, as he teased even lower with his probing tongue.

When she thought she couldn't bear the ache to have him inside her any longer, he rose up, quickly sheathed himself with a condom, then came back to her and slid an arm under her hips.

"I want you so much, Eloise…you and only you. Let me love you now…let me, please…."

"Oh, yes, now…please," she replied, opening herself to him in every way she could.

He claimed her with a single swift stroke, but waited then, holding back just a little longer until she had adjusted to the depth of his possession. Acknowledging her desire for more, she lifted her hips and entreated him softly with the murmuring of his name.

Bill needed no other spur to finish what he'd begun, taking both of them quickly to a heart-shuddering completion that had Eloise clinging to him, crying out as tears of joy filled her eyes.

She had never thought to feel so loved again, or to be so completely fulfilled physically and emotionally as she was in those moments. And even knowing that there was no promise of permanence in their time together—that real life would inevitably get in the way of what they'd shared—didn't make those moments any less heartening.

As she curled close to Bill, eyes on the flickering fire, and matched her gradually slowing breaths to his in the afterglow of their lovemaking, she savored a new sense of peace. And though she knew that it wouldn't last forever, she wished with all her heart that it could.

Chapter Eleven

Making love with Eloise had been all Bill hoped it would be, and more. So much more, in fact, that afterward, holding her close in his arms, he wasn't sure what to say or what to do. He didn't want to risk spoiling in any way the new affinity they'd found, something he could have too easily done with a single wrong word.

Together in his bed, souls as well as bodies bared, they were two simple, ordinary people who had freely shown how much they cared about each other. They had set aside all other concerns and all other responsibilities to focus on their own needs and desires. And the result had been truly wonderful.

But Bill knew that maintaining the same degree of self-indulgence beyond the weekend wasn't going to be possible for either one of them. Other demands on their time and attention would surface. And specific issues would force a separation as they pursued divergent goals.

He had certain principles to uphold and so did Eloise. He couldn't expect her to back down on the stand she'd taken any more than he could back down on the stand he had taken.

But just then Bill didn't really want to consider what might happen when they returned to New York City Sunday afternoon. He wanted to pretend for a little while longer that he was a regular old Joe enjoying the company of his lady-love in a secluded cottage by the sea.

"You're awfully quiet," Eloise murmured into the silence.

Tipping her head back against his shoulder, she gazed at him inquiringly. In the pale glow of lamp and firelight, her eyes wide, her lips slightly kiss swollen, and her hair uncharacteristically mussed, she looked sexy as hell. But there was also a vulnerability about her that tugged at his heart.

She had given herself to him without hesitation, revealing the depth of her desire without reservation. Such openness couldn't have been easy for someone as naturally reserved as she had always been. Which only served to underscore how solicitous he had to be toward her.

He didn't want her to feel, even for a moment, that being there with him—making love with him—had been a mistake in any way. And she might easily assume that without a little reassurance from him.

"I was just trying to hang on to…this," he said, hugging her closer still. "I was afraid I might only be imagining that I had you here with me, and if I opened my mouth and said…anything, you'd disappear."

"Oh, I assure you I'm very real and I'm not going

anywhere anytime soon—at least not of my own volition.''

She smiled up at him sleepily, then pressed a kiss to the hollow at the base of his throat, making him growl under his breath.

''I can't tell you how happy that makes me.''

Reaching out, he cupped her face in one hand and bent to share yet another deep and wholly intimate kiss with her. She shifted against him enticingly, sliding one leg over his in obvious invitation. His own body stirred with a renewal of anticipation, and once again he felt years younger, not to mention much more virile than he would have ever thought possible.

Breaking off their kiss with a low groan of frustration, he smoothed a hand over her hair as he eased away just a bit.

''Hold on to that thought, okay? I'll be right back.''

''Hurry,'' she urged as he slipped out of bed and headed for the bathroom. ''It's lonely here without you.''

He cleaned up quickly, then took a few extra minutes to stoke up the fire, adding several logs from the basket by the hearth. Outside darkness had fallen and the rain still came down, though more lightly if the tapping against the windowpanes was any indication. But he couldn't have been any cozier, or any more at peace, than he was there with Eloise.

She welcomed him back into bed with open arms, then shivered delicately as she snuggled close to him.

''Mmm...I hope you didn't catch a chill,'' she said.

''Only a little one, but I'm warming up already,'' he assured.

''That's good...''

168   *PRINCE OF THE CITY*

Rolling onto her back, she pulled him with her, arching under him again with undisguised invitation.

"I want you, Bill Harper," she murmured, sounding just the slightest bit surprised. "I want you...desperately."

"Again?" he asked, his own tone gently teasing. "How greedy you are, Ms. Vale."

"Only on extremely rare occasions." She nibbled delicately at his neck, then moved her hand between their bodies, capturing him in an intimately insistent grip.

"I must say that if this is one of those occasions, your...discrimination is, um, excellent," he muttered, a definite catch in his breath.

"May I please have one of those foil packets?" she requested prettily, the torment of her fingertips almost more than he could bear.

"Oh, yes, you most certainly may," he agreed, hesitating not at all as he shifted onto his back.

With a wicked smile, Eloise followed after him and soon had him completely, and delightfully, at her mercy.

Dressed in navy wool pants and an ivory turtleneck sweater, Eloise stood by the wall of windows overlooking the beach early Sunday afternoon, sighed quietly, then took a sip of coffee from the bright green mug she held.

She couldn't believe how quickly the time had passed. Actually, she didn't want to believe her weekend with Bill was coming to an end already. And the weather—the one legitimate reason they would have had to stay another night at the cottage—wasn't cooperating at all.

While flakes of snow were falling from the overcast sky, they weren't thick enough, and the temperature wasn't low enough, for them to cause any problems on their drive back to the city.

Not that Eloise wanted to miss being home for her sons when they returned from Washington, D.C., that evening. And staying another night at the cottage would have only postponed her inevitable parting with Bill, not eliminated it altogether.

But, oh, how she wished their magical time alone— loving each other without inhibition—didn't have to be over just yet.

It seemed as if they had only begun to be truly at ease with each other and the new level of intimacy their relationship had attained. Making love with Bill, sleeping in his bed, sharing a shower stall with him, had all taken some adjustment, on her part, at least.

She had been alone for the past three years, except for her sons, and she hadn't had to allow for an adult male's quirks in all that time. Not that she'd minded allowing for Bill's quirks once she'd discovered them, she thought with a smile.

When he snored she simply nudged him onto his stomach. And she'd quickly learned not to join him in the shower until the water had warmed up, allowing him to be invigorated by the initial icy blast all on his own.

But now they were going to have to go their separate ways again. And they would have to take up the lives they lived apart, often—especially for Bill—in public view. Moments like they'd shared together at the cottage would not only have to be planned well in advance, but stolen from job—and in her case, family—responsibilities that had to have top priority. And they would have to be very careful about where and when—if—they were seen together, too.

Unlike here, where they'd been totally alone, free to

do whatever they wanted whenever they wanted without worrying that someone might somehow distort their relationship in order to use it against them in some way.

They had dozed together for a while after making love a second time early yesterday evening. And when they'd awakened, they had taken a long, luxurious shower, then wandered down to the kitchen to fix a very late supper of salmon, salad and fresh strawberries.

They had eaten on the sofa in front of the fire, watching an old movie on television just like an old married couple relaxing on a Saturday night. But later, back in Bill's bed, they had made love yet again, their physical desire for each other still at an almost insatiable, honeymoon stage.

They had also slept late that morning, and made love one more time before finally agreeing that they would never make it back to the city before her sons arrived home if they didn't get up and get dressed. They had eaten breakfast first—the last of the strawberries and bagels Bill found in the freezer. Then he had sent her upstairs to shower and dress while he tidied up the kitchen one last time.

He was upstairs himself now, and finished with his shower, Eloise assumed, since the sound of water running had stopped a few minutes ago. Her signal to start the dishwasher, she also remembered, swallowing the last of her coffee then reluctantly turning away from the windows and crossing the living room to the kitchen.

She would have loved another walk on the beach, but that would have to wait until another time. If there happened to be another time, she reminded herself as she sat on the sofa and kicked off her loafers then drew her feet up under her.

Last night's fire was now just a pile of glowing embers to be shoveled into a bucket along with the ashes from the fireplace in Bill's bedroom, and set safely outside before they left. But Eloise's memories of the time she'd spent sitting there with Bill, talking together during the afternoon, and then later well into the wee hours of the morning, were fresh and alive.

They had discussed so many things—likes as well as dislikes—revealing quite a bit about themselves in the process. But they hadn't mentioned the one issue waiting to stand between them again once they'd returned to New York City.

They had set it aside, calling a truce, but now what would they do? Eloise wondered.

She had divulged so much about herself to Bill. He had to know now that she wouldn't have put so much of her time and energy into an organization unless she'd had total faith in its value to society. He also had to know how much the preservation of that organization meant to her. And he must understand that he and he alone had the power to see that Manhattan Multiples continued to receive city funding.

He had already shown her in so many ways how much he cared for her. That being the case, wouldn't he then want to do everything he could for her? Wouldn't he make her happiness a top priority in his life? And knowing how happy it would make her, wouldn't he see to it that Manhattan Multiples continued to receive city funding?

Even after making love with Bill, sharing the kind of closeness only two truly caring adults can share, Eloise wasn't sure of the answers to her questions. He had admitted to wanting her desperately seventeen years ago. But he had also admitted that his political aspirations had been first and foremost in his life back then, as well, and he'd simply assumed she'd go along with whatever he chose to do.

Was he making the same assumption now? Did he think that their physical intimacy had been a stepping stone to attaining her acquiescence across the board to whatever decisions he made in the future?

If so, he would be sadly disappointed, and so, in fact, would she. She couldn't turn her back on Manhattan Multiples just to make life easier for Bill.

She wouldn't.

And she was afraid Bill felt the same way about his proposed cuts to city funding. He believed they would help more people than they would hurt—never mind that her organization would definitely be one left hurting.

"You're looking rather pensive," Bill said, his mild tone, obviously meant to sooth, startling her all the same. "Not thinking unhappy thoughts, are you?"

"Trying not to," she hedged, attempting to dredge up a smile for him with only limited success.

They still had a few hours to spend together, and she didn't want to spoil that time with worries she could attend to just as easily the following day. She had trusted Bill enough to be sexually intimate with him, and he had been a kind, gentle, thoughtful lover. Surely she could trust him to be equally kind, gentle and thoughtful about something as close to her heart as he knew Manhattan Multiples to be.

He had assured her that he would never intentionally do anything to hurt her, and he hadn't yet. Until he actually behaved badly toward her, what could it hurt to have a little faith in him and the continuation of his consideration toward her?

"I admit I haven't been feeling all that chipper myself this morning." He set the ash bucket on the hearth, moved the fire screen out of the way, then knelt down and grabbed the little shovel hanging on the tool rack. "I kept trying to think of ways for us to just disappear for a week or maybe a month. Then I'd remember you have three teenage sons in need of mothering, and I'm the mayor of New York City. We'd have search parties hot on our trail before we crossed the state line."

"Funny you should say that. I was wishing the same thing," Eloise admitted, pushing off the sofa and padding over to kneel down beside him on the hearth. "I had a wonderful time the past couple of days. Being here with you has been like a dream come true, but like most dreams, it seems as if it's ending before it's even really begun."

"My sentiments exactly. We haven't even had two full days alone together," Bill muttered ruefully. "And who knows when we'll be able to slip away on our own again. Although I've been thinking maybe we could bring the boys out here for a couple of days over the Thanksgiving holiday."

He glanced at her, a hopeful glint in his bright blue eyes.

"Thanksgiving?"

Eloise made no effort to hide her dismay, though it wasn't with Bill's suggestion that they bring her boys to the cottage over the holiday weekend. She had been so caught up in wrangle over city funding, and then her very personal reacquaintance with Bill, that she'd completely forgotten about Thanksgiving, now only a couple of weeks away.

"I always fix a big turkey dinner, but as of today I'm totally unprepared," she explained as Bill continued to eye her questioningly. "We eat late so we can go to the big parade, too. The boys have always loved standing on the sidewalk watching all the floats go by. In fact, I love it, too. And I've learned to buy a smaller turkey so we can also eat dinner at a reasonable hour.''

"Hey, I'll be riding on a float in the parade,'' he said, grinning as he turned away again to finish cleaning out the fireplace.

"Somehow I'm not surprised. But then the mayor always rides on a float in the Thanksgiving Day parade, and you are the mayor.'' She grinned back at him, then added casually after a moment's hesitation, "Any plans for dinner afterward?''

"Actually, no—no plans at all. And if you're inviting me to join you and your sons after the parade, consider your invitation accepted with pleasure,'' he replied, surprising her in the nicest possible way.

She had been sure someone had already included him in his or her plans for the day. But Thanksgiving was a holiday devoted more to family than friends, and while Eloise had her sons, Bill had no family of his own anymore. Like her, he was an only child and his parents, older when he was born, had both died years ago.

"Well, yes,'' she admitted laughingly. "I was getting to that. I'd love for you to have dinner with us.''

"Then I will most certainly plan to be there.'' Leaning toward her, he gave her a swift kiss on the lips as if to seal the deal. Then he scrambled to his feet and extended a hand to help her up, as well. "Let me get rid of these ashes so we can hit the road. Do you have your bag packed and ready to go?''

"Packed,'' she acknowledged, meeting his gaze. "But nowhere near ready to go. I really do like being here with you.''

"We'll come back again. If not at Thanksgiving, then

another time, because I really like being here with you, too.''

This time when Bill kissed her, there was nothing swift about it at all. He took his time, turning the mating of their mouths into an intimate pledge for the future. And when he finally broke away and turned to dispose of the ash bucket, Eloise had to force herself to let him go.

They would never leave the cottage, much less head back to the city, unless they continued to remind themselves and each other of all the other responsibilities they had. They were mature adults, after all, not feckless teenagers.

Although when she was in Bill's loving arms Eloise had to admit she didn't feel anywhere close to the fortysomething years she knew herself to be. She felt as if she were standing at the brink of an excellent adventure unlike any she'd ever experienced in the past.

And she believed in her heart of hearts that she couldn't have had a better companion to share whatever fun awaited her than she had in Bill Harper, mayor of New York City or not.

While he checked over the cottage one last time, making sure that the French doors had been securely locked and the dampers in the fireplaces had been closed, Eloise poured the rest of the coffee into a thermos to take with them on the drive home, then rinsed out the pot. Bill's caretaker couple would finish the cleanup the following day, although there was little to do except empty the dishwasher and change the linens in the bedrooms and baths.

"All set?" Bill asked at last.

"All set," she agreed, resigned to the inevitable, but sending a smile his way all the same.

She'd had much too good a time to let a little momentary sadness spoil what remained of the day. And she was sure she would return to the cottage with Bill again.

He had all but promised as much, hadn't he? And she was feeling much too optimistic about the future, *their* future, to give any thought at all to the myriad problems that could come between them in the meantime.

Snowflakes continued to drift from the sky as they started their drive back to the city. But as Eloise had foreseen, the weather wasn't bad enough to cause any real problems. Even when the snow changed to a heavier fall of icy rain and sleet closer to the city limits, Bill was still able to drive at a reasonable though somewhat slower rate of speed.

It being a Sunday, traffic would have been light to start. And with less than perfect weather across the region, a lot of people had obviously opted to stay off the roads, as well.

They arrived at Eloise's building with time to spare before her sons were due home. The school had arranged for the students to be dropped off at their respective residences by the bus company upon their return from D.C., and Eloise had been told to expect her sons about six o'clock at the earliest, seven at the latest.

Since it was only four, and Eloise was reluctant to part with Bill just yet, she asked if he'd like to come up to her apartment for a while.

"I'll understand if you can't, though," she added shyly. "You probably have a lot to do to get ready for the week ahead."

"Nothing that can't wait a few hours more," he assured her as he retrieved his Official City Business parking pass from the SUV's glove box.

"Hey, must be nice," she said, waving a hand at the printed cardboard placard he positioned conspicuously on the dashboard.

"Rank occasionally still has a few privileges," he agreed with a mischievous grin.

"Oh, yeah, just a few," she teased as the doorman came up to the SUV with an umbrella, ready to escort her into the building.

"Of course, you wouldn't know about that, would you?" he teased right back, then greeted her doorman with a gracious smile and a comment about the cold, wet weather.

Upstairs, Eloise hung their coats in the entryway closet and turned to lead Bill into the living room. She had fully intended to put on a little soft music, light the gas logs in the fireplace and offer him a glass of wine. A few steps into the living room, however, Bill caught her by the hand, pulled her into his arms and proceeded to kiss her quite thoroughly.

She hadn't really planned to take him by the hand and tug him toward her bedroom…until that kiss. And the thought of stripping off her clothes, then tumbling into her bed with him hadn't crossed her mind, either…until that kiss. But the intimate coaxing of his lips on hers, his tongue and teeth adding to the sensual fervor, undid her completely.

Surely she hadn't become addicted to making love with Bill Harper, and most certainly she wasn't obsessed with him and the pleasure he so gladly gave her. It was just that they were so…good together. And who knew when—even if—they would have another chance to be alone like this again.

Curled close in his arms afterward, the unbelievable

heat of their passion having brought them to a swift and wanton climax, Eloise could hardly catch her breath.

"That was…incredible," Bill muttered. "*You* are incredible…the most incredible woman I've ever known."

"I didn't really mean for this to happen," she admitted, a rueful chuckle underlying her words.

"Well then, sweetheart, I can hardly wait until you *do*," he teased. "Although I may need oxygen before you're finished with me."

"No, no," she protested. "I didn't invite you up to the apartment just to seduce you."

"Then I'd say it's a damned good thing I decided to seduce you, isn't it? Think of what we would have missed," he said.

Then he trailed a line of hot, wet kisses along the curve of her neck as if to refresh her memory, even though it wasn't necessary.

"I just didn't want you to think I was…insatiable or anything," she murmured breathlessly.

His wry laugh, soft and deep, made Eloise smile and helped to ease her embarrassment.

"And that would be a bad thing?" he asked.

Sliding a finger under her chin, he tipped her face up so that she was forced to meet his gaze.

"Well, no, I suppose not."

"I hereby solemnly swear that it will be our secret," he assured her, an extremely satisfied smile tugging at the corners of his mouth. "In fact, it's going to give me untold pleasure knowing, as I now do, that hidden under the tailored clothes, low-heeled shoes and pearls you seem to favor is one very sexy little lady."

"Once again I must take exception to your use of the word *little*, but otherwise I'm flattered that you find me sexy," she replied.

"Oh, Eloise, sweetheart…you have no idea…."

Reluctantly, aware of the time passing and her sons' imminent arrival home, they dressed again and returned to the living room. There, Eloise picked up where she'd left off just after they'd arrived. She turned on the CD player and lit the gas logs in the fireplace while Bill found the wine, corkscrew and glasses right where she told him to look in her kitchen.

"So what's on your agenda for tomorrow?" he asked when they'd curled up comfortably on the sofa.

"I'm not sure," she hedged, not really wanting to bring Manhattan Multiples into their conversation even in a vague or indirect way. "We usually have a staff meeting first thing Monday morning, and that sets the pace for the rest of my day, and usually the rest of my week. What about you?"

"Staff meeting, too." He twirled his glass so the ruby-red wine glinted in the firelight, and silently stared into the crackling flames as if aware that he was treading near dangerous ground.

They were perfectly happy together—peaceful and serene—until they talked about their respective jobs. Then the conflict between his goals and hers couldn't be ignored. Nor could the ramifications that conflict had for their future together.

They might want to pretend to be any old married couple, Eloise thought, but the fact was, they weren't. Whatever she had on her agenda for the following day, it could, and likely would, throw a monkey wrench into the works of Bill's agenda, and vice versa. And was that any kind of foundation on which to build a permanent, loving relationship?

Sadly Eloise thought not as the silence stretching between them lengthened disconcertingly.

"Well…" Bill began, then swallowed the rest of his wine in a single gulp and set his glass on the coffee table. "I thought I'd stick around so I could say hello to your sons, but I'm thinking maybe I'd better go before I wear out my welcome."

Eloise knew that if she protested Bill would likely stay. Carl, John and Henry would be happy to see him. She could order pizza or Chinese food for dinner, then she and Bill could hear all about the events of their weekend trip to Washington, D.C.

But she couldn't bring herself to say the words that would keep him from leaving as he stood and shoved his hands in the pockets of his jeans. All she could do was stand, too, and offer politely to get his jacket from the closet in the entryway.

Much as she hated having their time together end on what seemed like a sour note of sorts, she didn't want to risk stirring up even more acrimony between them by having him stay any longer.

"I really had a wonderful time," she said yet again as he slipped into his jacket.

"So did I, Eloise," he replied, digging his leather gloves and keys from his pockets.

"I'm glad."

She was on the verge of offering him her hand in a farewell gesture, but he didn't give her the chance to be so impersonal. With a low growl of something akin to frustration, he reached for her and pulled her close for one last, exquisitely luscious, lingering kiss.

Eloise tried to resist but couldn't seem to do it. And then, just as she was rethinking her decision to send him on his way, he let go of her, turned on his heel and walked out the door without another word.

Well, fine, she thought, pressing her fingers to her tenderly swollen lips. Just go. See if I care.

But she did care, rather desperately, as a matter of fact, standing alone in the quiet of her penthouse apartment. She once had been happy there on her own, but now she felt only a sense of remorse for what she wanted but would likely never be able to have.

No matter how she wished they could have a future together, she couldn't see any way it was going to be possible. They weren't an ordinary couple with relatively ordinary problems. He was the mayor of New York City and she was a prominent socialite, and they were locked in a very public battle. They had totally different goals that couldn't be easily reconciled. But he had all the power, and if he used it against her, she would never be able to trust him again.

Chapter Twelve

Staying focused proved to be an almost impossible task for Bill on the busier than usual Monday morning that followed his weekend with Eloise.

A major part of the problem was lack of sleep. Memories of all the hours they'd spent together were fresh in his mind, and thus too vivid to be easily ignored even if he'd wanted to during the long restless night he'd tossed and turned alone in his bed. And he hadn't.

He'd allowed himself to savor each and every recollection he'd had of the moments when they'd talked, walked on the beach and enjoyed the simple meals they'd prepared. And of course, most tantalizing of all were the images in his mind of the lovemaking they'd shared.

The sheer physicality of it had taken his breath away even in memory. But more heartening had been the depth of emotion they'd experienced in each other's arms. There had been no holding back between them, either in his bedroom or in hers. They had made love openly, honestly, intimately, giving and taking in equal measures. They had bonded in a way that spoke not only of hearts meshing, but also souls, and not in a transient way, but for all time.

But then the realities of their separate lives had intruded along with the conflicting goals they had no longer been able to set aside. Battle lines had been drawn between them again. Surely, though, there had to be some way for them to cross those lines. And surely, too, they would be able to find a common ground where each of them could stand by their chosen beliefs and fulfill their responsibilities and still be together as a couple.

His faint but growing hope that he could find some reasonable and agreeable resolution to their discord over city funding cuts had also distracted him most of the day.

As he had emphasized during his morning meeting with Francis Wegner, the president of Construction Services, cuts had to be made to funds formerly designated for nonprofit organizations in order to help rebuild the city. But maybe, as he had discussed with Charles Goodwin, the reporter from the *Daily Express,* during his interview that afternoon, there might also be some way the blow to the nonprofits could be softened.

Aware that a little research was in order if he had any hope of attaining that previously unthought-of solution, Bill had asked Wally Phillips to compile as much information as possible on the organizations likely to suffer most seriously as a result of his proposed cuts. He had also asked that Wally include in each report the services provided by the organization and the number of people who would be affected by the organization's possible closure.

Stacks of file folders, separated according to services provided, had begun appearing on his desk just after noon and had grown steadily ever since. Having brought his interview with Charles Goodwin to a satisfactory conclusion, Bill was now ready to get down to work.

But first he took a moment to call the florist he'd visited discreetly a little earlier to make sure the flowers he'd ordered for Eloise had been delivered as requested.

Yes, the clerk assured him, the crystal bowl filled with yellow roses and tiny white carnations should have arrived at her office within the past hour or so. The clerk would let him know for sure when the driver finished his rounds and returned to the shop.

Bill had debated about sending the flowers most of the morning. He and Eloise had parted the previous evening with a slight but still noticeable chill creeping between them. His fault for bringing up the workday ahead and asking her how she'd planned to spend it.

He had felt so comfortable with her, so completely at ease that he hadn't remembered until too late that her chief occupation of late had been battling his proposed budget cuts. With the truce they'd called for the weekend almost over, of course she'd been thinking about the work she had yet to do. And that meant picking up right where she'd left off Friday evening as soon as she got to her office Monday morning.

Reminded of their conflict, she had begun to pull away from him emotionally, best evidenced by her sudden use of the polite but distant tone he disliked so much. He hadn't wanted to leave just then, but he'd thought it wise to give her the space she seemed to need while he was still at least somewhat ahead.

He had wondered later if he should have stood his ground and forced the issue out in the open. They could have each argued their points yet again, then they could have kissed and made up just like most couples did after a disagreement.

But with Eloise's sons due to arrive home at any time, it had been too late by then to go through that particular routine. In fact, he'd even talked himself out of calling her when he got back to Gracie Mansion. He'd been sure that she'd be too busy with her sons to welcome any further distraction from him.

Bill had also thought about calling her first thing that morning. But Francis Wegner had arrived early and stayed longer than anticipated. Before he'd known it, Wally was taking orders for lunch, and suddenly a personal trip to the florist to order flowers for her had seemed like the best possible idea under the circumstances.

But even considering the short note he'd sent with the roses and carnations, would she think the gesture too dispassionate? They had been intimate with each other, extremely intimate, and her response to his lovemaking had meant more to him than he could ever say.

Would she think because he hadn't called her that he'd taken their mutual show of affection for granted? Would she assume, mistakenly, that he'd gotten what he wanted from her after a seventeen-year delay, and was now ready to move on?

The possibility that Eloise might allow either of those ideas to enter her mind had Bill staring out the window at the leaden sky, a sinking feeling in the pit of his stomach. Again he envisioned himself attempting to cross a minefield, every step he took carrying with it the potential to blow him out of Eloise's life forever.

"Okay, sir, here's the last of the reports you requested on the nonprofit organizations coming under the gun."

Wally Phillips strode into Bill's office without knocking, as usual, and set a stack of eight or ten file folders on the one corner of his desk still remaining empty.

"I've sorted them out as you asked, too. Family related services are here." Wally tapped one pile of folders. "Substance abuse programs here," he continued with another tap of his hand on another pile of folders. "Food banks and meal kitchens here, and miscellaneous here. Are you sure you want to review all of the reports on your own? I can have a couple members of our staff work on some of them and write up short synopses for you."

"I know, but I'm the one making the cuts. I want to find out for myself exactly who's going to be affected and how badly. And if there's any way to minimize the damage to the most worthwhile of the organizations, I want to be sure I find it before I proceed any further with finalizing the necessary cuts."

"Which you promised to announce within the next couple of weeks," Wally reminded him. "By the first week of December at the latest, if I'm not mistaken.

"Don't worry, Wally. I plan to keep that promise," Bill assured his chief of staff. "So let me get started on my research, all right?"

"Of course, sir."

"And hold my calls."

"All of them, sir?"

"I'll talk to Ms. Vale."

"I had already taken that for granted." Wally eyed him with a knowing smile as he backed out of the office. "Family services in the stack of file folders to your right," he reminded Bill. "I believe that's where you'll find the necessary information on Manhattan Multiples."

Then, as Bill growled an expletive, he beat a hasty retreat.

He should have known his chief of staff would see right through his sudden interest in detailed information about the nonprofit organizations due to have their city funding cut, Bill thought. But Wally also had to know that he would go out of his way to be equally fair to all the organizations concerned. He had too much integrity to do anything else.

Yes, Eloise was important to him, and if he could find a way to help Manhattan Multiples, along with other similar organizations, survive his proposed cuts, he would. But he wouldn't play favorites just to please her. That would demean everything he'd worked for all of his adult life, and that was one thing he couldn't do.

No matter how much he cared for Eloise Vale, he still had to be able to look at himself in the mirror every morning. And if he couldn't do that, he wouldn't be much good to anyone including her.

"Special delivery for Ms. Eloise Vale," Allison advised.

Her voice was bright and cheerful as she walked briskly into Eloise's office that dreary Monday afternoon.

Drawn none too gently from her reverie by her assistant's untimely and unknowing intrusion, Eloise spun around in her desk chair and eyed Allison less than agreeably.

She had spent most of the day in a dismal mood, staring out the window at the gray clouds and falling rain. Normally she would have welcomed any excuse to refocus her attention on something other than her own personal problems. But she had actually been enjoying her miserable wallow in a rather perverse way. And she would have preferred to be done with it at her own pace, however lethargically that pace proved to be.

"Oops, sorry…" Allison halted in midstride, her smile fading as she saw the expression on her boss's face. "I didn't mean to disturb you, but these flowers were just delivered for you and I thought you'd like to have them right away. I should have buzzed you on the intercom first. I know that, and I'm sorry…."

"Allison, sweetheart, stop apologizing," Eloise instructed kindly, dredging up a reassuring smile for the younger woman.

"I know you've had a lot on your mind all day," her assistant continued, her tone still contrite.

"Yes, well…" Eloise waved a hand, her gesture dismissive. "That's no reason for me to be in such a grumpy—"

Her gaze fell at last on the small, round, crystal bowl filled with yellow roses and tiny white carnations that Allison held, and her voice trailed away. She knew immediately who had sent the delicately lovely flower arrangement. Only one person had the incentive to present her with such a tribute.

Eloise's smile faded as a hot blush swiftly suffused her face. No one knew that she'd spent the weekend with Bill Harper, not even her sons. And certainly no one knew how her relationship with him had changed during that two-day period. But by sending her flowers he could easily stir up suspicion.

Although, Eloise noted, the envelope Allison also held was sealed, so only she, as the recipient, and the hopefully discreet florist would know whose name was on the accompanying card.

Suddenly, unexpectedly, she felt the prickle of tears in her eyes. She had been so sure for so much of the day that she had run Bill off for good last night. In fact, considering the way she'd behaved toward him just before he'd left her apartment, she wouldn't have been surprised if he chose never to contact her again.

One minute she had been curled up in her bed with him. The next minute, figuratively speaking, she had been on the verge of extending her hand to him in a cool but polite attempt at dismissal not only of him, but also of all they'd shared together.

All she had really had to cling to until now was the kiss he'd given her before he'd walked out her front door. And even that kiss had carried with it more than a hint of goodbye and good riddance—both well deserved.

She had thought Bill would call her later Sunday night, then couldn't blame him when he didn't. Nor was she surprised that he'd made no effort to contact her that day.

Each time Allison had buzzed her to announce an incoming call, Eloise had jumped in nervous anticipation, hoping it was he finally breaking his silence. Finally, however, she'd convinced herself—as she'd stared at the gray clouds hanging low over the city—that she had pushed him away one time too many.

Bill had been honest with her, and oh, so loving. He had more than earned her trust, as well. Yet she kept raising the hoop of unrealistic expectation, then waiting for him to jump through it even though he would have had to turn his back on his own principles to do it.

He had never asked for a similar show of devotion

from her. In fact, he had shown great consideration for her cause and respect for her faithfulness to it.

Wasn't that kind of deference proof in itself of the true depth of his feelings for her?

"Would you like me to put the flowers on your desk?" Allison asked, her voice soft and tentative.

"Yes, please." Reaching out, Eloise shifted stacks of papers to make a space for the crystal bowl.

"There's a card, too," her assistant added as she set the envelope beside the bowl.

"Thank you, Allison." Eloise drew a steadying breath and managed to offer the younger woman another re-assuring smile. "And I apologize again for being so short with you a few minutes ago."

"I understand completely. It can't be easy having to start work on next year's budget without knowing, one way or another, how badly we'll be affected by the funding cuts."

"It's actually almost impossible," Eloise admitted. "The way things stand right now—including the capital we have on hand from the fund-raisers we've held, but excluding city funding completely—I can afford to pay rent on our office space or I can pay our employees' salaries and provide about half of our current services.

"Luckily, our lease is up in March, and I'm reasonably sure I can manage to pay all of our bills until then. Maybe in the meantime, I'll also be able to find a less expensive place where we can relocate. Otherwise I may have to run Manhattan Multiples out of my apartment, at least temporarily. That's where the organization started thirteen years ago, and while it's not where I'd hoped to be now, it's better than having to close down altogether."

"Manhattan Multiples is so much more than a place,

Eloise. It's the people, like you, who make it worth-while, and that's always been the case. We all know how much of yourself you've put into the organization, and we're all behind you one hundred percent. We'll find a way to keep offering our services to the women who need them, and among all of us, we have lots of apartments we can use as bases for our various operations if need be.''

''I know we will,'' Eloise agreed, thoroughly heart-ened by her assistant's enthusiasm. ''I've always thought of Manhattan Multiples as the people, not the place. With all of us working together, I know we'll be able to keep going no matter what happens.''

''We all feel the same way, Eloise. We've all gone through so much together already. We'll get through whatever fallout comes with Mayor Harper's budget cut, too. We are women, and we are strong,'' she stated with a proud tip of her chin.

''We are, indeed,'' Eloise agreed.

''That said, I'd better get back to work on those Please Send Money letters so we can get them out in today's mail.''

Alone again, Eloise drew the sealed ivory vellum en-velope across her desk with a cautious fingertip.

There was no guarantee that Bill's message would be one she wanted to read. He could have sent the flowers as a means of establishing closure to their personal re-lationship. He hadn't sent red roses, after all—the sym-bol for love. But weren't yellow roses a symbol of hope?

Maybe he'd wanted to let her know that he hadn't given up on her. There was only one way to find out.

Slowly Eloise pealed back the flap on the envelope and withdrew the plain ivory vellum card tucked inside of it. Scrawled with black ink in Bill's distinctive script were a few simple yet intimately meaningful words: "Then, now and for always—Bill"

Again tears pricked at Eloise's eyes as an overwhelming sense of relief washed over her. She hadn't realized how deeply she'd feared the possible loss of him in her life until that moment. Nor had she realized how much his continued allegiance would boost her sagging spirits.

Bill could have easily given up on her. She'd certainly given him enough reason with her constantly waffling behavior. But he hadn't, and from the words he'd written, the pledge he'd made, Eloise couldn't believe he ever would unless she gave him no other choice.

And if he cared for her as much as he'd indicated, then she also had reason to hope that she could still win him over to her way of thinking about his proposed cuts to the funds she needed so desperately for Manhattan Multiples. All she had to do was let him know that she'd gotten his message and she trusted it to be true.

Quickly Eloise searched her Rolodex and found the telephone number for the direct line into Bill's office at city hall. She dialed it herself without hesitation, not wanting to give Allison any reason to connect the crystal bowl full of flowers she'd just received to the mayor. She also figured she'd have a much better chance of getting through to Bill on her own rather than via a third party, even one as determined as her assistant could be.

"Mayor Harper's office. Wally Phillips speaking. How can I help you?"

Eloise was only momentarily disconcerted by Bill's assistant's greeting. Even Bill's private line would have to be monitored, especially if Bill was on another call or attending a meeting.

"Hello, Mr. Phillips. This is Eloise Vale. May I please

speak to Mayor Harper if he isn't busy?'' she requested in her most polite, yet most assertive tone of voice.

"Of course, Ms. Vale. Hold on just a moment while I let him know that you're on the line."

Eloise waited not even a full sixty seconds, then Bill's rich, masculine voice flowed over the telephone line. Her heart was immediately warmed by his evident delight in taking her call.

"Eloise, hello. It's so good to hear from you," he began. Then he hesitated as if he were wondering if what she had to say to him would indeed prove to be good, before adding, "I've been thinking about you all day."

"I've been thinking about you, too, Bill," she acknowledged.

"Good thoughts, I hope."

"For the most part, yes," she replied, hoping he could hear the smile in her voice. "I just received the flowers you sent. They are beautiful. Thank you so much."

"I wasn't sure if you liked yellow roses, but I thought that no matter what they would add a little cheer to your day. Especially since it's still so gray and gloomy outside."

"I love yellow roses, and you're right—they are cheerful. They've really brightened my day in more ways than one."

"Did you get the card I sent, as well?" he asked with just the slightest hint of concern.

"Yes, I did, and I appreciate the message."

"I meant what I said, Eloise. I hope you can believe that. We may not agree on everything, but can we at least agree that we care about each other? And can you believe that nothing I've done in the past or will do in the future is intentionally meant to hurt you?"

"I believe you, Bill. And I apologize for my behavior

last night. I did exactly what I'd agreed not to do when we talked together at the cottage. I acted like a brat again, shutting down on you without an explanation and, I'm afraid, making you feel that you'd done something wrong when all you really did was ask about my plans for today.''

''That probably wasn't the smartest conversational tack I could have taken, all things considered,'' he admitted with a rueful chuckle. ''But I wasn't really thinking at the time. If I had been I would have remembered that you've spent a lot of time lately working against me.''

''Not against you personally,'' she hastened to assure him. ''Just certain proposals you've been promoting that I can't support.''

''I understand completely,'' he replied. ''And I hope you understand that those proposals I've been promoting aren't intended to hurt you personally, either.''

''Yes, I understand, but your proposals *are* forcing me to face having to make some painful choices in the weeks ahead.''

''Please don't do anything drastic just yet, okay?''

''Okay…'' she agreed, though tentatively.

''I haven't made any definite decisions, one way or another, about the budget cuts, and I won't until after the Thanksgiving holiday. I've come up with some ideas that might just result in a solution to the city-funding problem we can both agree upon.

''I'm not making any promise, Eloise. I can't in good conscience. But will you trust that I *am* keeping your best interests in mind, and that whatever I decide, I will try to be as fair as I can to everyone involved?''

''I can do that, too,'' she said, feeling more optimistic than she had in almost a year.

She had always considered Bill trustworthy, at least in her more rational moments. It was only when fear about the future of her beloved Manhattan Multiples made her crazy that she lashed out at him in a flurry of unwarranted doubt and disappointment.

"Remember that truce we had over the weekend?" he continued, a teasing note creeping into his tone.

"Quite well, in fact," she replied. "I rather enjoyed it, too."

"So did I." He chuckled again making her blush even though she was alone in her office. "Any chance we could reinstate that particular truce for the next couple of weeks?"

"A very good chance if that's what you'd like to do," she agreed, making no effort to hide her eagerness.

"That's one thing I would *definitely* like to do, but only one of many."

"Then consider our truce officially reinstated," she said, then added teasingly, "What else would you like to do?"

"See you again face-to-face just as soon as I can."

"We have a date for Thanksgiving dinner at my place," she reminded him.

"That's almost two weeks away. Any chance we could get together before then? Maybe take the boys out to dinner and a movie?"

"Is that possible for you to do without getting mobbed by your faithful supporters?"

"Well, it's not totally impossible with a little advance planning. How about Saturday night?"

"I'm free on Saturday night and I'm pretty sure the boys are, too."

"Let's make it a date, then."

"Okay, let's do," Eloise agreed with a sense of anticipation that had her grinning ear to ear.

"I'll get back to you with the details."

"Sounds good to me."

"Talk to you later tonight?"

"Yes, please…later tonight."

"Bye, then…"

"Bye…"

Eloise had just cradled the receiver and was still smiling when both Allison and Josie appeared side by side in her office doorway. Both wore identically serious expressions on their faces, laced heavily with concern, and perhaps even a slight trace of fear.

"What's wrong?" Eloise asked as she pushed away from her desk and stood up.

Any lingering happiness she'd felt following her conversation with Bill faded immediately, replaced by a sudden sense of anxiety. Neither Allison nor Josie were the type to make mountains out of molehills. They wouldn't appear to be so distressed without good reasons.

"We received an Express Mail envelope from the post office a few minutes ago. It was addressed to all three of us—you, Josie and me," Allison explained. "I opened it, of course, since I open all of your mail. Inside I found three envelopes like this one, each addressed to one of us."

Allison crossed Eloise's office and handed her a plain white business envelope with her name printed on the front of it in block letters.

"We opened our envelopes and the letters inside were identical, as I imagine yours will be, too," Josie continued.

"So our letter-writing nut case has decided to target

you, too," Eloise muttered angrily, ripping open her envelope and pulling out the badly typed letter tucked inside it.

If you rich bitches don't let my wife alone I'll fix it so you won't be able to cause trouble for anybody else. This is your last warning. Stop interfering with my business. I have a gun and I know how to use it.

There was no signature, of course. That made the missive even more chilling. It could have come from anyone just about anywhere in the city.

"I immediately checked with our local post office. They told me it had been put into a drop box in upper Manhattan yesterday morning with postage stamps attached. The return address is a vacant lot in East Harlem."

"So there's no way we can track down the sender?" Eloise asked.

"Not with what we have here," Allison replied.

"And we haven't had any recent clients who have complained about serious marital problems or an abusive spouse?"

"The only one in the past six months to have had a major problem with her spouse is Leah Simpson. But he walked out on her before she came to us for help. To my knowledge, she hasn't even mentioned him since the babies were born," Allison said.

"I just talked to Leah Friday afternoon," Josie added. "All she said then was that she'd like to come back to work here the Monday after the Thanksgiving holiday if that's all right with you."

"Yes, that's fine with me," Eloise agreed.

She was momentarily distracted by the thought that Leah Simpson would need all the work experience she could get the next few months in case the Manhattan Multiples budget had to be trimmed as much as she feared it would. Then, eyeing the letter she still held between her thumb and forefinger in acknowledgment of how distasteful she found it, Eloise resolved to worry about Leah and the rest of her employees another day.

Just then she had an anonymous crazy man to contend with—a crazy man who no longer seemed quite as harmless as she had originally believed him to be. Especially if he had a gun and the determination to use it against her or anyone else associated with Manhattan Multiples.

"As for this nonsense," she continued, keeping her tone light and dismissive to ease Allison's and Josie's concerns. "I'm calling the police and then I'm going to have a little talk with the Martino brothers.

"First thing tomorrow morning we're going to have another staff meeting, too. I want everyone here to be extra vigilant from now on. And I want anyone who appears to be even the slightest bit suspicious reported to Frank or Tony immediately, and then a call placed to the police, as well.

"We're not going to take any chances and we're not going to give anyone the benefit of the doubt, at least for the time being. I also want the two of you to take precautions while you're here—no more coming in early or staying late until further notice. Understood?"

"Yes, of course," Allison and Josie chorused in unison.

"And you won't keep odd hours, either, will you?" Allison asked.

"No more odd hours for me, either," Eloise assured

them. "Now let me call the police while you track down Tony for me, okay?"

"Okay, boss," Josie replied in a teasing tone, then added on an inquiring note, "Nice flowers. Do you have a secret admirer?"

Eloise blushed as her gaze fell on the bouquet of yellow roses and spicy scented carnations.

"Something like that," she hedged, unable to lie to the two young women, but also unwilling to reveal anything about her relationship with Bill to them just yet. "Now let me make that call."

She gestured with her hands, shooing them out of her office, and to her relief they left without any further questions. They did, however, whisper to each other and giggle as they walked down the hallway, causing Eloise to smile, but only for an instant.

She had to call the police and she had to talk to Tony and then she planned to head home to spend a little time with her sons. And, she added, to wait for Bill's call.

She didn't want to tell him about the anonymous threats she'd been getting, especially the latest one. She didn't want to add to his concerns when he already had a lot on his mind, much of it to do with her. She simply wanted to sink into the strength and reassurance of his quiet, considerate, oh-so-sexy masculine voice, and be reminded that in him she could find a safe harbor if she needed one. All she had to do was trust him, and she did.

Chapter Thirteen

"Bye, Mom."

"Bye, Mom."

"Bye, Mom."

The sound of her sons' high-spirited voices echoing around her in triplicate made Eloise smile as she and Bill stood together on the sidewalk outside a posh apartment building on Lexington Avenue.

She wouldn't have been nearly as happy as she was to let her boys join a friend of theirs for a late movie and sleepover that Thanksgiving night if she'd been on her own. But with Bill as eager as she for a little time alone together—at last—she hadn't thought twice about allowing Carl, John and Henry to accept the early-evening invitation issued, she knew, from parents who had likely been badgered all day by their lonely only child, already bored with the holiday.

"Please be on your best behavior," she cautioned as

she gave each of her sons a hug and kiss on the cheek. "Mr. and Mrs. Shaw aren't quite as used to rowdiness as I am."

"We'll be good, Mom," Carl assured her.

"Yeah, Mom, you know we will 'cause we always are," John added pragmatically.

"You're right. You always are," she agreed.

"Don't forget—we'll be home in time for dinner tomorrow night," Henry reminded her.

"I'll be waiting for you," Eloise vowed. "Just be sure to let me know if you have a change of plans, though."

"We will," they chorused, then headed toward the entrance of the apartment building where the doorman, obviously forewarned by the Shaws, waited to greet them.

"Are you sure you don't want to go upstairs with them?" Bill asked solicitously. "I don't mind waiting for you out here."

"I talked to Suzie Shaw on the telephone. There's no need for me to talk to her again, especially if it means leaving you standing on the sidewalk, alone in the cold. The boys are fine riding the elevator on their own. As they keep reminding me, they're *thirteen,* and I'm more overprotective than any of their friends' parents are."

Tucking her hand into the crook of Bill's elbow, Eloise turned with him to walk back to her apartment building several blocks away.

"I don't think you're that bad," he said, putting his hand over hers and giving it a squeeze.

"I don't think I am, either, at least not under normal circumstances. But it's my responsibility to look out for them. They're still boys, after all."

They walked at a moderate pace, enjoying the quiet of the evening now that they were finally on their own.

Though the temperature hovered just above freezing, the clouds and rain that had hung on drearily for the past two weeks had finally blown out to sea. The sky was now clear, and far above the buildings the moon shone in full splendor.

The day had been a hectic one for both of them. In fact, the past two weeks had been busier than usual, allowing them very little time together, and until now, no time at all alone.

They had gone out to dinner twice with her sons in tow, both times to quiet out-of-the-way neighborhood restaurants where Bill was duly recognized, greeted, then left to enjoy his meal with her and the boys in relative peace. The previous Sunday Bill had joined them for brunch at her apartment, too. Then they had rented movies to watch—all of them together—during the long, rainy afternoon.

She and Bill had talked on the telephone every night, as well, sometimes at such great length that Eloise had a hard time waking up the next morning. By mutual agreement they had totally avoided the subject of Bill's proposed funding cuts. But the specter of his inevitable and upcoming announcement hung over every word they spoke.

Just a few more days and she would know the worst, Eloise had thought yesterday afternoon. Although she continued to trust that Bill would find the viable solution for which he'd vowed to search almost two weeks ago— if he hadn't actually done so already.

She'd been tempted to ask him about it every time she'd talked to him. But she had held back, believing that he would at least inform her first of his final decision before he announced it to the public at large during the press conference scheduled for Tuesday morning.

Maybe he planned to do that tonight, she reasoned, now that they had a little private time together. Then again, maybe not. He had told her regretfully on Wednesday evening that he had to cancel their tentative plans to go out to his cottage over the holiday weekend. Some last-minute information regarding city budget allocations had come into his office late that afternoon and would have to be reviewed before his press conference.

Bill hadn't seemed to want to say any more than that, and Eloise hadn't hounded him about it. But she had heard the weariness in his voice, and she had been afraid that whatever new information he'd received, it didn't bode well for Manhattan Multiples.

"Cold?" he asked, putting an arm around her shoulders and drawing her closer to his side.

"No, surprisingly, I'm not." She looked up at him and smiled. "What about you?"

"Impossible as long as I'm with you." He bent and gave her a quick kiss on the lips. "You warm me, heart and soul."

"Oh, go on with you," she retorted, but she snuggled even more comfortably into his embrace.

They walked another block in companionable silence, then Bill spoke again.

"How about tired?" he asked. "You've had a busy day."

"Just a little," Eloise admitted after a few moments of consideration. "The boys had me up at the crack of dawn so we would be sure to get a prime place for viewing along the parade route. We had to be near the starting point so we'd be able to see most of it and still get home in time for me to put the turkey in the oven."

"I can't believe I actually saw you in the crowd," Bill commented. "But then, you were right up front and the boys were just rambunctious enough to catch my attention."

"That's certainly a polite way of saying that they were jumping around like little maniacs, shouting and whistling and waving at you with both hands," Eloise pointed out.

She smiled as she remembered her sons' excitement at seeing the mayor riding high above the crowd on his special float. They had been determined to get a wave from him and they had. So had she, for that matter, along with a wink she seriously hoped no one else had noticed in all of the hubbub going on around her.

"I'm glad they found a way to stand out in the crowd. Seeing all of you together made my day, and when you smiled and waved, too…"

He hugged her close for another quick kiss.

"I thought my dinner was the highlight of your day," she said with a pretty pout.

"Let me put it this way, then. Seeing you at the parade was the highlight of my morning, your dinner—which was excellent, of course—was the highlight of my afternoon."

"So there's nothing special left for you to look forward to this evening?" she asked with an inquisitive arch of her eyebrows as they walked toward the entrance of her apartment building.

"Oh, I wouldn't say that. In fact, Ms. Vale, I didn't say that," he replied, his voice dropping low and taking on a husky undertone that made her tummy flutter in a truly delightful way. "In my opinion, the best is yet to come, my love."

"You sound awfully sure of yourself, Mayor Harper."

"I'm thinking I have reason to be, Ms. Vale."

They paused in their bantering to greet the doorman

as he welcomed them into the building. Then they stood silently as they waited for one of the two elevators to return to the ground floor. One eventually did and an elderly couple Eloise didn't recognize exited without really looking at either of them.

Once she and Bill had stepped aboard and the doors had whooshed closed on them, he pulled her into his arms and kissed her just as thoroughly as she'd been hoping he would. To her delight he also managed to take off his gloves, unbutton her long black wool coat and slip his teasing hands under her red cashmere sweater.

"Guess what?" he murmured into her ear when he finally broke off their kiss.

"What?" she murmured in reply as she gazed up at him with a slightly inquiring smile.

"We're not only alone, we're alone in an elevator, and all I can think about is that little fantasy you mentioned when we were at the cottage." He bent his head and nibbled at her neck. "Want me to push the stop button?"

"Only if you can also think of some way to disable the security camera without, um…arousing the security guard's interest," she answered then giggled at the shocked look and the furious blush that immediately spread across his handsome face.

"Security camera?" He backed away from her and swiftly rebuttoned her coat again. "Why didn't you tell me sooner?"

"It was kind of hard to say anything until you'd finished kissing me," she replied with a wicked grin.

"Oh, lady, I haven't anywhere near finished kissing you. Although I'll wait until we're in the privacy of your apartment before I let my actions speak louder than my words."

"Good idea."

When the elevator doors opened at last on the penthouse floor, Bill grabbed Eloise's hand and pulled her down the hallway to her front door, forcing her to walk briskly to keep up with his longer strides. At her door he took her key and deftly inserted it into the lock.

When the door was finally closed and their coats tossed onto the padded bench in the entryway, he caught her hand again and led her to her bedroom without the slightest hesitation.

"I can't even begin to tell you how long and lonely the past two weeks have been without you," he said when they had discarded their clothes and snuggled together deep under the covers on her bed.

"No need to explain," she assured him as she trailed tiny, biting kisses over his chest. "I've missed you, too…desperately."

"I don't really want us to be apart the way we've been, but—"

"But it can't be helped," she cut in, placing a gentle, warning finger against his lips. "We both have certain…responsibilities we can't ignore right now. Maybe in a while our circumstances will change and we'll be able to…to…"

Unsure what direction their relationship might take in the days following Bill's press conference on city funding cuts, Eloise allowed her voice to softly trail away.

"Just be together," Bill finished for her. "Preferably living happily ever after."

"What a romantic you are," she quipped more lightheartedly than she felt.

She wanted a happily-ever-after life with Bill more than anything else, but the possibility of actually having it remained tenuous at best.

"Only where you're concerned," he said, cradling her face in his hands and kissing her tenderly on the forehead. "You make me feel like a knight in shining armor. Now if only I can find a way to rescue my lady love, all will be well in the kingdom."

"I'm not sure I actually need someone to rescue me. I've gotten pretty good at doing it myself."

"Hey, just because we couldn't fulfill your fantasy by making mad, passionate love in the elevator doesn't mean I should have to give up mine," Bill said.

"Okay, okay, rescue me, please...." Eloise teased.

"But you're not in any danger here."

"Then let me rescue you because you're very close to being in danger yourself."

"And why is that?"

"You're talking too much and personally I'm ready for action."

"Oh, yeah? You want action? I'll give you all the action you can handle and then some."

"Promises, promises," Eloise murmured.

Then she caught her breath as Bill burrowed under the bedcovers and put his mouth on her in a most deliciously inventive way.

Lying in bed with Eloise very early the following morning, Bill didn't want to think about anything except how grateful he was to be there with her. He wanted to stay completely in the moment.

He didn't want to remember the pain of losing her that he'd suffered in the past. Nor did he want to consider the choices he was going to have to make in the very near future.

But time was running out. He had made a commitment to certain principles and he couldn't, in good conscience, waffle now. His decision regarding cuts to city funding had to be announced within a few days. And he hadn't yet found a solution that would not only allow him to keep his promise to the people of New York in general, but also demonstrate to Eloise how important she, and by extension Manhattan Multiples, was to him.

He had hoped to come up with something by now, but so far he'd had no real luck. All of the nonprofit organizations he'd studied over the past few days offered necessary services. All had just as much right to city funding as Manhattan Multiples did.

Choosing one over another would be grossly unfair. It would also defeat the whole purpose of the across-the-board cuts he'd originally proposed. He had pledged from the very beginning not to play favorites, and even for his beloved Eloise, he couldn't, wouldn't, renege on that promise.

Granted he had some new information to review—stacks and stacks of it, in fact. But the prospect of finding an agreeable compromise was fading too fast for his liking.

He had asked Eloise to trust him, and she had. Now he wondered how she would react when he finally had to tell her that he'd have to let her down, after all.

Would she choose to believe as she had seventeen years ago that she wasn't as important to him as his political career?

More than likely, Bill admitted. And he wouldn't blame her. He'd been the one to remind her just last night that actions always spoke louder than words.

By cutting off all future city funding for Manhattan Multiples, he would be showing Eloise that he'd chosen to allow his personal concerns to take a back seat to his public concerns. He would also be setting a precedent, in her mind at least, for the future—a future she wouldn't want to spend with someone as untrustworthy as he would have become in her eyes.

"Are you awake?" she murmured as she stretched in his arms with a languorous sigh.

"Yes," he replied, tightening his hold on her.

Forcefully he willed away all the what-ifs that had been warring in his mind. Whatever happened within the next few days—whatever final decision he made—he wasn't about to let his worries ruin the little remaining time they had left alone together.

"Ready to get up?" she continued, then kissed the side of his neck invitingly.

"Not unless you are."

He stroked a hand over her breast, rubbing his thumb temptingly across her nipple. Then he moved his hand lower to tease her in a place even more wickedly sensitive.

"Not me...not at all."

She sighed softly, moving her legs apart to give him easier access.

"I was hoping you'd say that."

Smiling down at her, he tested her readiness with a probing fingertip and found her hot and wet and throbbing with a desire that matched his own.

"Mmm, and I was hoping you'd do...that..." She gasped as he bent his head and captured a nipple with gentle teeth. "And that...and...oh, yes...that, too...."

Much later, when they had both caught their breaths again and the sun had begun to peek through the slats of the window blinds, Eloise spoke, her tone much more tentative that it had been earlier.

"I know you said that you were going to have to work over the weekend. Does that include today, too?"

Bill thought of the new stack of file folders sitting on his desk in his office at Gracie Mansion and sighed inwardly. Then he thought about spending the day with Eloise, just the two of them on their own together for the next eight or ten hours—just until her sons returned home for the evening. And he chose what he wanted, needed, to do most.

"No, not today. Today I'm all yours, unless you've made other plans."

"Not a one." She smiled up at him, her eyes alight with expectation. "What would you like to do?

"Take a ride on the Staten Island Ferry," he replied without hesitation. "Then maybe take a walk in the Cloister Gardens. We could look at the Christmas decorations in the windows of all the big department stores, too."

"In other words, pretend we're tourists?" Eloise asked, seeming enchanted by the idea.

"Exactly."

"It's been so long since I've done any of those things," she admitted.

"Same for me. So, are you game?"

"Oh, yes, I'm definitely game."

They made a day of it—a day full of love and laughter that Bill would never forget. They showered and dressed and set off in high spirits, stopping at a deli for bagels and coffee to enjoy while they walked in the cold clear air, the sun warm on their faces.

They rode the ferry first, standing close together on the top deck where Bill enjoyed a surprising and welcome amount of anonymity. The Cloister Gardens were next on their agenda and relatively quiet that Friday after Thanksgiving when most people headed to the department stores to start their holiday shopping.

They ate lunch sitting on a park bench, munching foot-long hotdogs that tasted even better out in the fresh air. By the time they made it back to Eloise's neighborhood, the crowds on the sidewalks were thick and bustling. Viewing the department store windows took some doing, but they managed, laughing and teasing each other as they wove their way through the ranks of people so they could press their faces against the plate glass like a couple of kids.

They arrived back at Eloise's apartment building just as twilight had begun to fall. Her sons would be home within the hour, and no matter how much Bill wanted to stay into the evening, duty had finally begun to call out to him in the form of guilt pangs he found harder and harder to ignore.

Much as he didn't want his time alone with Eloise to end, neither did he want that day to be the last day she willingly spent in his company.

"I can't believe how much fun that was," Eloise said as they rode the elevator up to her floor.

Unlike the night before, Bill maintained a discreet distance between them. Not because he didn't want to continue the closeness they'd shared all day, but because he wouldn't be able to leave her at her door if he did.

"We do seem to have a good time when we're together," he agreed.

"I wasn't sure we'd be left alone as much as we were," Eloise admitted as they stepped off the elevator and started down the hallway to her front door.

"People can be pretty considerate sometimes. We had the bustle of pre-Christmas shopping in our favor, too. Everyone seemed to be paying more attention to their own concerns than they were to us. I haven't always been so lucky out in public, but I'm glad we weren't bothered today."

"So am I." As they paused outside Eloise's door, she fished her key from her pocket. "Would you like to come inside and have a glass of wine? The boys should be here soon, too. I could fix turkey sandwiches or something...."

"I would like nothing better than to stay awhile longer, but I'd better not. I really do have work waiting for me and a deadline of sorts looming, and I've played hooky long enough already."

Eloise's smile faded for an instant, then she made an obvious effort to put on a happy face again.

"No problem. I understand. Thanks for making yesterday and today so special for me, Bill."

"You're the one who made our time together special," he replied, smoothing a gentle hand over her hair. "I want a whole lot more of the same, too—time together, that is."

"Yes, so do I."

"I'll call you, okay? Later tonight..."

"Yes, later tonight."

This time when she smiled at him there was just the faintest hint of sadness in her eyes. She was trying so hard to believe in him, he knew. But she must have sensed his own waning confidence in his continued ability to warrant that trust.

There had to be a way, he told himself as he kissed her one last time hard on the lips, then turned and walked away.

And if there was, he was determined to find it so that he could have not only today with Eloise, but a whole lifetime, as well.

Chapter Fourteen

The photographs splashed across the front page of the Sunday edition of three major papers shouldn't have come as such a surprise to Eloise. In fact, once the initial shock had worn off, she realized that she should never have considered their outing to be as private as it had seemed.

They had been out in public all day Friday and Bill was the very popular mayor of the city they'd toured. Most people had been courteous enough to keep their distance, and that had made it possible for both of them to forget his celebrity status. Obviously they had also been so wrapped up in each other that they hadn't taken any notice of photographers, tailing them casually and snapping off an occasional shot of them here and there.

At least the photographs were tasteful. But then, she and Bill hadn't been overt in their public displays of affection. There was one picture of her standing beside

Bill on the top deck of the Staten Island Ferry, his arm around her shoulders. Another featured them walking hand in hand in the Cloister Gardens and a third showed them sitting on a park bench eating hot dogs.

The headline on one of the articles read "The Mayor Manhattan-Style," and the article itself was fairly bland. Basically it chronicled their personal tour of various popular city sites with a teaser or two about the possibility of a budding romance between the two of them thrown in for good measure. But there had also been a final paragraph that brought up the matter of the mayor's proposed budget cuts and how Manhattan Multiples, Eloise's own nonprofit organization, could be affected by them.

The article had ended with several questions posed to the reading public. Had Ms. Vale been successful in convincing Mayor Harper to continue funding to Manhattan Multiples during their outing? Would other organizations benefit, as well, if the mayor softened his original stance? And would Mayor Harper's plan to revitalize the city as a whole no longer be top priority? Inquiring minds wanted to know, but would have to wait until the mayor's press conference on Tuesday to find out.

Eloise was tempted to call Bill and ask him if he'd seen the photographs and read the articles in the Sunday papers. But she had promised the boys she would take them to the skating rink at Rockefeller Center, an annual outing they all enjoyed after Thanksgiving. And they were eager to get to the rink before the crowd grew too big. She and Bill had gotten into the habit of talking during the evenings, and they could do that Sunday night, as well.

As usual, she and the boys made a day of it. Carl, John and Henry took turns dragging Eloise round and round the ice rink until she begged for mercy. She was finally allowed to sit on the sidelines while they continued to skate on their own.

Eventually the boys had had enough themselves and they piled into a taxi for the second half of their annual ritual—a ride to E.J.'s Luncheonette where even Eloise pigged out on the best pancakes in town served all day long.

Home again, the boys headed for their rooms to finish homework in preparation for school again the following day. Seeing the message light blinking on the answering machine in her bedroom, Eloise pushed the button and listened as Bill's voice, calm and quiet, asked her to call him when she got home. She dialed the number of his private line at Gracie Mansion that he'd given her, and he answered on the second ring.

"Hi, it's me," Eloise said in reply to his somewhat distracted greeting, having no doubt that he would recognize her voice. "I just got your message."

"Hi, yourself. I forgot you were taking the boys to the skating rink today. Did you have a good time?"

"A very good time, although I'm sure I'm going to be sorry tomorrow that I didn't beg them to let me sit on the sidelines a lot sooner. My muscles are already beginning to ache," she admitted with a rueful laugh.

"Take two ibuprofen and call me in the morning," he teased.

"Oh, yes, I most certainly did," he replied, his voice shaded with a rueful tone.

"I was amazed at first that we didn't notice anyone taking pictures. But then I realized that we weren't really paying much attention to anyone but each other, and you are a celebrity of sorts around town."

"I know what you mean. And we *were* in public places that are regularly frequented by tourists carrying cameras. A reporter on the prowl wouldn't have had any trouble blending in enough to go unnoticed."

"Especially by two people who only had eyes for each other," Eloise repeated, smiling to herself.

"Like us."

Bill, too, seemed to be smiling, if the warmth she heard in his voice was any indication. But as he spoke again, Eloise heard a distinctive change in his tone that seemed to indicate he'd shifted into a more serious mood.

"There were some thought-provoking questions at the end of one article, too."

"The answers to which we'll all have on Tuesday, right?" Eloise asked, attempting to keep her own voice light and cheerful.

She hadn't mentioned his proposed cuts to city funding at all when they'd talked the past two nights. She had promised to trust him to do what he could for her and Manhattan Multiples, and she had vowed to herself that she'd wait patiently for him to advise her of his final decision. No badgering on her part to make what she knew to be a difficult choice even more stressful for him.

And Bill hadn't brought up the subject, either…until now.

"That's right…Tuesday," he agreed, suddenly sounding very weary.

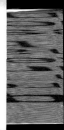

Eloise experienced a sinking sensation in the pit of her stomach. In her estimation, such obvious and unhappily expressed resignation on his part did not bode well for her cause. Had he come up with a workable solution as he'd hoped he would on Friday, he would have not only sounded much more upbeat, he would have also told her about the solution by now.

Still she couldn't help but hold out hope. He had shown her how deeply he cared for her. He had even indicated that he wanted them to share a future together. Surely he would do everything in his extensive power to make that possible, as long as he could also be fairminded about it.

"I'm thinking your day hasn't been quite as much fun as mine," she said. "Would you like to come over for a while, have a glass of wine, watch a little television, eat a turkey sandwich? I'm seriously pushing turkey sandwiches around here. If I'd been thinking straight Friday evening I would have sent you home with a bag of leftovers."

"I'd love nothing better than joining you for a glass of wine and a turkey sandwich, but I'd better not. I still have work to do before the press conference Tuesday and I have a feeling tomorrow is going to be level-ten chaos from start to finish. I'll take a rain check, though, if one's available."

"Sure, another time would be fine. I'll probably have

wouldn't like him very much at all for what he would be doing to Manhattan Multiples.

"Maybe next weekend, then," he suggested, sounding hopeful.

"Yes, next weekend might be nice," she agreed, though she couldn't muster up much enthusiasm and no longer felt much like trying.

As if sensing her change of mood, Bill allowed his own weariness to surface again.

"I'd better get back to work, then. Talk to you tomorrow?"

"Yes, we can talk again tomorrow. Good night, Bill."

"Good night, Eloise."

She didn't have an especially good night. She had managed for the past two weeks to convince herself that her trust in Bill was well placed and everything would be all right. But after cradling the receiver that Sunday night, all the doubts and concerns she had kept at bay raised their ugly heads, demanding her attention.

She had gone over and over the alternate ways in which she could keep Manhattan Multiples going if city funding was cut. She knew all too well what she would have to do. The *if* was what weighed her down as she tried to sleep.

Eloise had always believed that knowing was infinitely better than not knowing, that facing reality was wiser than living in a fantasy world. She could only hope that she would feel the same way come Tuesday morning.

As it so happened, she didn't have to wait quite as long as she'd thought she would. Monday, not Tuesday, became her day of reckoning. Braced for the worst as she'd assumed she was, when it became the reality she'd thought she was prepared to face, she ended up feeling as if her knees had been knocked out from under her.

The day had started out well enough. At the Monday-morning staff meeting, they had all welcomed Leah Simpson back to work. Eloise had also reminded everyone to be on the look-out for strange men lurking around the office.

Allison and Josie, along with some of the other members of the staff, had teased her about the photographs and accompanying articles in Sunday's papers. Eloise had fended off their questions by admitting that although she and Mayor Harper had spent some time together the Friday after Thanksgiving, they had simply been getting to know each other better, professionally, while touring the city.

She had doubted anyone really believed her, but she didn't care. She didn't owe anyone a more detailed explanation. And she wasn't about to give one when she might not have any relationship at all with Bill Harper in another day or two.

Luckily Allison had diverted attention by putting a hand on her tummy, going very still and getting a dreamy look in her eyes.

"What is it?" Josie had asked.

"I just felt the strangest sensation. Like tiny butterflies fluttering inside of me," Allison had said. "Do you think...?"

"Oh," had gasped Eloise, knowingly.

Eloise had smiled knowingly.

"Yes, I think it's the twins. They're letting you know they're having a little playtime."

The sonogram Allison had had almost two weeks ago had proven Eloise to be right. Her assistant was having multiple-birth babies—twins, a boy and a girl, Dr. Cross suspected, although he wouldn't be sure until her pregnancy was a little further along.

"Is this the first time you've felt them move?" Josie asked, her eyes alight.

She was quite used to her own baby's rolls and tumbles, and obviously enjoyed knowing that Allison would now be enjoying a similar reminder that she'd soon be a mother, too.

"Yes, it is." Allison had grinned, then went still a second time. "Oh, there they go again. I can't believe it. I have to call Jorge."

"By all means, call Jorge," Eloise had urged her, glad to have someone else taking center stage. "And, Josie, I'd like you to call these people and tell them I'll get back to them as soon as I can."

She had handed her receptionist several message slips. Each noted a call from someone Eloise hadn't wanted to talk to until she had a better idea of what additional funding she'd need and how she hoped to acquire it if Manhattan Multiples' city funds were cut.

Alone in her office, Eloise went to work and by noon she'd sketched out plans for a possible spring fund-raiser to be held after Easter. She had also called a real estate agent who had been supportive of Manhattan Multiples in the past and asked her to start looking for smaller and more affordable office space into which she could move Manhattan Multiples sometime after the first of the year.

Liz Cooper had sounded confident that she could find exactly what Eloise needed. Eloise wasn't sure Liz had understood her new definition of affordable, but at least the search was on. Once Eloise had eliminated a few properties on the basis of cost, she had no doubt Liz would get the message without need of an elaborate explanation.

Leah had stopped by Eloise's office during her lunch hour, too. She had wanted to show off her tiny daughters who had spent the morning quite contentedly in the Manhattan Multiples nursery while Leah resumed her duties as a file clerk. Mother and babies had seemed to be thriving, and Leah was effusive in her thanks to Eloise for the warm welcome back to work she'd received earlier at the staff meeting.

Eloise had also asked Leah about the husband who had abandoned her. Leah said that he had called a few times after the babies were born, but she'd made it clear that she wanted nothing more to do with him.

Left alone again, Eloise had just finished the sandwich she'd been eating at her desk when Allison buzzed her on the intercom.

"Are you busy?" her assistant asked, her voice sounding somewhat strained.

"Not really. Why do you ask?"

"There's something I think you should see—an article in today's edition of the *Daily Express*. I came across it just now."

"I have time to read it now."

"I'll be right there, then."

As good as her word, Allison appeared in the doorway of Eloise's office within a few moments. In her hand she held a copy of that day's edition of the *Daily Express*. On her face was a look of deep concern that stirred a sick feeling in the pit of Eloise's stomach.

"The article is on the front page of the business section," Allison explained, carefully folding back the paper to the appropriate page. "It's written by Charles Goodwin. He's the reporter who interviewed Mayor Harper a couple of weeks ago. He's written this article as a follow-up."

Eloise remembered the original article detailing Goodwin's interview with Bill. It had been fairly written, presenting the mayor's reasons for proposing cuts in city funding for nonprofit organizations in a way that had helped even Eloise understand better why he thought them to be necessary.

The current article was most certainly a follow-up as Allison had said. In it, Charles Goodwin claimed to have posed some questions to Bill's chief of staff, Wally Phillips, regarding Bill's relationship with her as evidenced by the photographs and accompanying articles in Sunday's papers. He also asked about the possibility that funding for Manhattan Multiples would not be cut because of his obvious personal interest in her.

According to Mr. Phillips, contacted at his home Sunday afternoon, Goodwin stated:

Funds previously earmarked for Manhattan Multiples will be cut along with those funds formerly directed to other nonprofit organizations already listed by the mayor. The scope of the funding cuts will be outlined in detail at the mayor's press conference scheduled for Tuesday morning at ten o'clock. Mayor Harper will also present his plan for revitalizing the city of New York, a plan that is said to include salary increases for firemen and police officers, sanitation and other city workers. Strengthening the city as a whole has been and continues to be Mayor Harper's primary goal, and he is prepared to make whatever difficult choices are necessary to achieve that end.

Lowering the newspaper to her desk, Eloise looked up at Allison as the reality of what she'd just read began to sink into her consciousness. Apparently Bill had made his decision, and he had made it before he'd talked to her Sunday evening. Yet he hadn't warned her in advance so she'd be prepared.

Funds for Manhattan Multiples will be cut...will be cut...will be cut...

The words played over and over in her mind, affecting her painfully. Bill had asked her to trust him and she had. She'd also known he would follow his conscience, but she had expected, at the very least, that he would tell her about his decision before announcing it to the city.

What had he hoped to gain? A few nights together playing bump and tickle as payment for the hurt she'd caused him seventeen years ago? She would have never thought he could be that cruel. But then, how well had she really known him?

A few days over a period of a few months in someone's company half a lifetime ago and an equally few number of days over a period of a few weeks in that same someone's company more recently did not provide the wealth of information necessary to make sound judgments. Sadly, she hadn't had the sense to realize that she'd been placing all her confidence in someone who now seemed more like a stranger. But she realized it now, and the pain of it made her want to crawl away and hide under a rock.

"Oh, Eloise, I'm so sorry," Allison murmured as if she were aware of how deeply the knife edge of pain had been driven into her boss's heart. "I'll just let you..."

Hesitantly she took a step back, then halted when Eloise raised a staying hand.

"No, wait, Allison...please."

Drawing a steadying breath, Eloise willed away the hurt and the anger that had also begun to blossom deep inside of her. She didn't have time to mourn for the loss of something she'd never really had. Nor did she have time to find a way to avenge herself against the man who had duped her completely.

She did spare a moment to hope that Bill Harper would eventually get his comeuppance. Then she marshaled all of her energy in a positive direction. She had other people to consider, people like Allison and Josie and Leah who depended on her to be strong enough and sensible enough to hold Manhattan Multiples together in a crisis.

She had hoped she wouldn't have to do it on her own—had, in fact, hoped that Bill Harper would see how necessary all the nonprofit organizations were to the city and find a way to make the cuts less drastic. But that possibility had fallen to the wayside. She was on her own again as she had been for a long time already. But that didn't mean she was without resources, the most important of which being her indomitable force of will.

She met Allison's questioning gaze and dredged up a reassuring smile that seemed to bolster not only her assistant's sagging spirits, but her own, as well.

"What can I do to help?" Allison asked in a stronger, more certain tone of voice.

"It won't be long before word of Goodwin's article starts to spread through the office, if it hasn't already. Confirmation of the funding cuts is upsetting, of course. But it's not totally unexpected. Still, it's going to be worrisome to everyone here, and I'd like to ease concerns just as much as I can before panic mode sets in. So, Allison, please ask everyone to gather in the conference room for another staff meeting in thirty minutes.

and tell anyone who can't make the meeting to see me before they leave for the day.''

"The conference room in thirty minutes," Allison repeated. "I'll get right on it."

The meeting went as well as Eloise had hoped it would. So did her personal talks with those few employees who weren't able to attend the meeting. The general mood was rather glum, of course. She hadn't been the only one hoping Manhattan Multiples' city funding wouldn't be cut. But she managed to reassure everyone that she was a very long way from being ready to close the doors.

She mentioned the various options she'd been considering and made certain that all of her employees understood that their jobs would be secure and their salaries paid for at least the next six months. While there was still concern about the long-term future, there was also a noticeable determination among all of the people working for Manhattan Multiples to keep the organization going so that its services would be available as long as possible.

The mayor's televised press conference was scheduled for ten o'clock the following morning, and at Eloise's suggestion it was agreed that everyone who could would meet then in the Manhattan Multiples lobby. There they could watch together and hear as a group—dedicated to beating the odds—exactly what he had to say.

As she tucked a few papers into her briefcase late that afternoon, Eloise tried to be grateful that the roller-coaster ride of uncertainty she'd lived with the past five months was finally over. The worst was about to happen, but she, along with her industrious staff, was ready to face it and move on.

The conference had been not only moving, but also

truly gratifying. Everyone associated with Manhattan Multiples had agreed with her belief that it wasn't the place but the people who made the organization worthwhile. And the people would go on however and wherever they could.

The buzz of her intercom startled her so badly she knocked her briefcase to the floor. She had told Allison she wouldn't be taking any more calls that afternoon. In fact, she had thought her assistant and Josie had already closed up shop and were at the reception desk together, only waiting to leave the building until she was ready, as she now was, to go with them.

"Yes, Allison?"

"I know you asked me to hold your calls, but Mayor Harper is on the line and he's being very insistent about wanting to talk to you," her assistant said in a hushed voice.

Eloise debated what to do for a good thirty seconds. She could talk to him and get what would definitely be their final conversation over and done. But she didn't have the energy to deal with him just then. She wanted to go home, soak in a hot tub, put on her woolly robe, curl up in front of the television and watch mindless sitcoms with her sons while eating Chinese take-out.

She had already been just about as strong as she could be in any one day. Mayor Harper would have to wait until tomorrow when her emotional batteries would hopefully be fully recharged.

"Did you indicate in any way that I'm still here?" she asked, her decision made.

"I told him you were unavailable to take calls," Allison replied.

"Good girl," Eloise approved. "Give me a few seconds to get out of my office, then tell him I'm gone for the day which will be technically true.''

"Okay, Eloise."

Retrieving her briefcase from the floor then grabbing her purse and coat, Eloise walked quickly to the reception area.

She arrived just in time to hear Allison say ever so politely, "I believe Ms. Vale has gone for the day, sir. She's not in her office, after all. Can I take a message for her?"

There was a pause during which Allison listened raptly to the voice at the other end of the line. Then she said, "I'll do that. Thank you, sir."

Pushing the disconnect button, she looked up at Eloise with a puzzled expression on her face.

"He asked me to tell you first thing tomorrow morning that you shouldn't believe everything you read in the papers."

"There are a lot of things I shouldn't have believed," Eloise admitted wearily. "The least of which is what I read in the papers. Now let's get out of here before the telephone rings again."

Of course, it did as they walked toward the double glass doors.

"The voice mail can take a message," Eloise said, halting Josie before she could turn back to the desk. "Go home, both of you. Give your husbands hugs and kisses and enjoy the rest of the evening. And don't show your pretty faces here till ten o'clock tomorrow morning. We'll pick up the pieces and start over then, okay?"

"Okay," they agreed in tandem as they reached the bustling sidewalk. "See you tomorrow, Eloise."

"Yes, tomorrow," she replied with a smile and wave of her hand to send them on their way.

Bill had suspected that Eloise asked her assistant to say she'd gone for the day when she was actually still at the Manhattan Multiples office. He'd had that suspicion confirmed when he called her at home a little more than an hour later and one of her sons answered the phone.

After a polite exchange of greetings, Henry had gone off to find Eloise, then come back on the line a few moments later to say she couldn't come to the phone just then. Bill had asked Henry to tell her to please call him back as soon as possible. He had even left the number of his private line at Gracie Mansion so she would have it readily at hand.

He had waited almost two hours without hearing from her. Not that he'd expected he would, but he had held out a smidgen of hope that for once she'd be willing and able to give him the benefit of the doubt.

He knew the reason for her silence as well as he knew his own name. He had seen Charles Goodwin's article in the business section of the *Daily Express* late that afternoon. And he'd figured it was a good bet Eloise had seen it, too, and believed every word she'd read to be absolutely true.

What she obviously hadn't factored into the equation was that *he* hadn't made the statements quoted in the article. His chief of staff had been the one to say that funds for Manhattan Multiples would be cut in the same manner as funds for other nonprofit organizations, and that had been true Sunday night. But Wally had also said that details concerning how the proposed cuts would be made would be outlined during the press conference Tuesday morning.

Nothing definite had been decided when Wally had taken it upon himself to answer Goodwin's questions. It had been an understandable attempt to nip in the bud unfounded rumors of favoritism stirred up by the press they'd received the previous weekend. And as far as Bill had been able to determine from the calls he'd received from various supporters, it had worked.

Apparently, Eloise had misread the article, though. She had likely seen the words *would be cut* and understood them to mean *had been cut*. She had jumped to every possible wrong conclusion as a result. And she had decided that she didn't want to hear anything he had to say in his own defense.

Well, he would just see about that, Bill thought as he hung up the phone after a third attempt to call her got him only her answering machine. He had changed into jeans and a sweater when he'd gotten home earlier. All he had to do was grab his leather jacket, gloves and scarf and head out the door.

He didn't bother calling his driver. He was too tense to sit quietly in the back seat of the limousine, and he was too distracted to drive the SUV himself. Maybe he would calm down enough by the time he reached Eloise's apartment building that he wouldn't be tempted to remind her that she was acting like a brat yet again.

The doorman recognized him, of course, and greeted him respectfully.

"Is Ms. Vale expecting you, sir?" he asked.

"Yes."

Not true, but he wasn't letting a doorman, however conscientious, stop him now.

"I only asked because your name isn't on the residents' guest list for tonight."

"A last-minute arrangement. It probably slipped Ms. Vale's mind. Ah, here's the elevator. I'll go on up."

"Um, okay, sir. I'll just let her know—"

The elevator doors closed, cutting off the last of the doorman's comment. But Bill knew what he'd been about to say. He was going to buzz Eloise and advise her that she had a guest on the way up to her apartment. He had hoped that she wouldn't be forewarned even that much but, in fact, he had to count himself lucky that he'd managed to slip onto the elevator without being stopped. New York doormen at buildings like Eloise's could be real bulldogs when it came to guarding the residents.

She wasn't waiting for him with the door open and a smile on her face. But then, he hadn't expected the luck he'd had getting so far to last. He could only hope she was averse enough to causing a scene that she hadn't called the building security with instructions to escort him out.

He paused in front of her door, drew a breath, then reached for the brass knocker and gave it a couple of good, sharp raps. Eloise must have been standing right behind the door because as soon as the sound stopped echoing in the hallway, she spoke just loud enough and distinctly enough to be heard through the barrier she insisted on keeping between them.

"Go away."

"Not until we have a little talk."

"We don't have anything to talk about."

"Not through a closed door. Let me in, Eloise."

"No."

Bill wanted to pound his fist hard against the wooden doorframe in frustration. Why did she always have to believe the worst of him without even hearing what he had to say? After all the time they had spent together, after all the intimate moments they'd shared, was she still unable, or perhaps simply unwilling, to trust him?

He deserved better than that from her. But if she didn't know that already, he had to face the possibility that she never would. And he wasn't about to spend the rest of his life trying to prove that he was worthy to someone who should have already realized it long ago.

Unable to hide the sudden weariness that washed over him, Bill spoke to Eloise through the closed door one last time.

"I really need to talk to you, Eloise...please."

"No, Bill. Now, just go away."

"If that's what you want, fine. But I won't be coming back."

"That's probably best."

Conceding defeat, Bill turned away from her door and walked back to the elevator. No sound of a lock turning or a voice calling out halted his progress.

And when the elevator doors slid open, he stepped inside without a backward glance.

By the time he'd reached the ground floor, he had managed to paste a pleasant expression on his face. He said good-night to the doorman and walked back to Gracie Mansion the way he'd come, his pace equally fast.

He wanted to read through his speech one last time before tomorrow. Then he was going to try to get at least a few hours of sleep, although how successful he'd be was debatable.

He might want to put Eloise out of his mind and even, at that moment, out of his heart. But some things were easier thought than done.

Chapter Fifteen

As ten o'clock Tuesday morning approached and the members of her staff began to gather in the Manhattan Multiples lobby, Eloise encouraged everyone to help themselves to coffee or tea and pastries or bagels from the trays she'd had delivered from the neighborhood deli an hour earlier.

Reinforcing the camaraderie among all those who kept her organization running had become her top priority for the day. She was more determined than ever to make the best of a bad situation, and she didn't intend to be deterred by the sleepless night she'd had.

Oddly enough, worries about Manhattan Multiples hadn't been the cause of her wee-hours tossing and turning. She already had plans in place, ready to activate, that would maintain the status quo during the first quarter of the following year when the effects of the funding cuts would first be felt. She knew she could continue to provide most of the organization's services until the end of March, though some would have to be scaled back. She hoped, too, that by the end of March she would be able to find a place to relocate. And by knocking on enough corporate doors, she would likely be able to increase private funding, as well.

No, it hadn't been Manhattan Multiples that had kept her awake most of the night, Eloise thought as she greeted Allison and Josie and urged them to try the cherry-cheese rolls. It had been the memory of Bill's final words, spoken just before he'd left her.

She had told him to go away because that was what she'd been sure she wanted him to do. And he had after several similar urgings from her as she'd stood resolutely behind her apartment door. But his parting shot had left her feeling as if a rug had been pulled out from under her.

I won't be coming back, he'd said, so calmly and quietly that Eloise had known he'd meant it—in no uncertain terms.

Only then had she been hit by the reality of what she'd wrought. And she'd wondered ever since if she'd made the same kind of mistake she'd made seventeen years ago—condemning Bill without giving him the chance to plead his case.

Though what he could have said to restore her trust in him she had no idea at all. There had been the cryptic message he'd left with Allison yesterday afternoon. *Don't believe everything you read in the papers.* But why would his own chief of staff tell a reporter that funds for Manhattan Multiples would be cut if it weren't true? Wally Phillips could lose all credibility by prevaricating to the press. He would also have done the mayor the kind of disservice that would have gotten him fired, as well.

It had been sometime after midnight when Eloise had gone in search of the copy of the *Daily Express* she'd brought home with her. Nothing new leaped off the page at her. Charles Goodwin's article read exactly the same as it had that afternoon. What had changed, however, was her interpretation.

With her defenses down, Eloise had seen immediately that Wally Phillips's statement had been more general than specific. He hadn't said funds for Manhattan Multiples *had* been cut, but rather that they would be cut in a manner similar to cuts to other nonprofit organizations. He hadn't given any details, either. He'd merely said they'd be forthcoming. And Bill had indicated Sunday night that he was still working on those details—long after Charles Goodwin had interviewed Wally Phillips.

That, Eloise had finally admitted to herself, had to have been why Bill wanted so desperately to talk to her. He had assumed, rightly, that she'd jumped to certain conclusions upon reading the article. And he'd wanted to put her mind at ease by telling her…what?

Had she not been so stubborn, not to mention so justifiably angry and upset, at least to her way of thinking, she would already know. Instead she had run Bill off for good and always. Which would be just as well if he *had* betrayed her trust. But if he hadn't—

"Eloise, the mayor's press conference is about to begin," Allison said.

Drawn from her reverie, Eloise allowed her assistant to lead her to the front of the small crowd now forming a semicircle around the television set positioned atop a chest in the lobby's sitting area.

The local network station flashed its Breaking News

logo onscreen as an announcer advised that the regularly scheduled program was being interrupted so the mayor's press conference could be televised live. Amidst the flash of cameras and the rustle of notebooks being opened by the reporters in attendance, Bill walked up to the bank of microphones positioned at the top of the front steps of city hall.

He was dressed in an elegantly cut dark-gray pin-stripe suit, white shirt and burgundy-red tie. To Eloise he looked not only heartachingly handsome, but also incredibly weary. Until he gazed out over the crowd of reporters and flashed his trademark grin. Then he exuded nothing but quiet confidence in himself and the budget-cutting decisions he'd chosen to make for the welfare of his beloved city and its people.

"Ladies and gentlemen," he began, his voice warm, his tone encouraging. "Thank you for giving me this opportunity to outline my plans for next year's budget for city funds. As you know, I have been faced with some tough choices, and I have made every effort to be fair about the future allocation of those funds.

"As you know, too, my primary goal has been the revitalization of our city and the general welfare of its residents as a whole. Initially it seemed that the only way to acquire the funds necessary to achieve my goal was to incorporate those funds that had previously been earmarked for various nonprofit organizations operating throughout the city. After much consideration, however, I realized that our nonprofit organizations provide a wealth of services to our citizens, and cutting off completely the funds they've come to depend on would be a mistake.

"In looking at our various nonprofit organizations, I discovered that in many cases, very similar, but autonomous, organizations provide the same services at twice the cost of a combined organization. It is my belief that by joining similar organizations and pooling their resources, services could continue to be provided with a much lower percentage of the city funds than formerly budgeted.

"For example, we have several meals programs, each serving a small area of the East Village, and each operating out of a its own location. By coordinating the programs in such a way that they can be run out of two main locations, city funding required could be cut by two-thirds without cutting services.

"Another example is Manhattan Multiples, an organization that provides services for women expecting multiple-birth babies. It has come to my attention that a similar organization, Brooklyn Babies, also offers services to pregnant women. By joining forces and pooling their resources, these two stellar nonprofit organizations would require only half of the city funding they now receive independently.

"The same is true of our many substance-abuse programs—"

Eloise sat in stunned silence as she realized what Bill had been saying. He had found the solution necessary to maintain Manhattan Multiples as a viable entity. And it was a solution she might have found herself if she hadn't been so busy ranting and raving about Bill's funding cuts the past few months.

She was familiar with the organization known as Brooklyn Babies. They differed from Manhattan Multiples only in that they offered more general services to all pregnant women rather than specialized services geared primarily to women expecting multiple-birth babies. Joining forces and pooling resources with them was definitely doable, especially if it meant they would still receive some city funding.

"Eloise, did you hear what Mayor Harper said?" Allison asked, her voice filled with excitement. "We're not going to lose our city funding after all, at least not completely. I've heard about Brooklyn Babies, too. The organization is about half our size but it has an excellent reputation."

All around the lobby, equally enthusiastic comments were being exchanged among her staff members.

"Yes, Allison, I heard what he said. He's certainly come through for us and for a lot of other nonprofit organizations, as well," she replied.

To herself she added, *just as he promised me he would.*

The sense of remorse Eloise felt was almost overwhelming. She had misjudged him totally, and as a result she had turned her back on him just as she had seventeen years ago. How she wished she hadn't been so willfully set against him last night. And, oh, how she wished she hadn't let him walk away from her with the promise that he'd never come back.

He wouldn't, either. Not when he'd asked her to hear what he had to say and she'd blatantly refused. Not when she'd thought the worst of him and had had no qualms about letting him know it. And certainly not when she'd let him believe she never wanted to see him again.

He was more than capable of taking a hint, and her behavior toward him last night had gone well beyond intimating that their personal relationship was over.

She could go to him, though. She *had* to go to him, if for no other reason than to thank him for all he'd done on behalf of the nonprofits, and to try to apologize for treating him so badly last night. *Try* being the operative word, since she was fairly sure there wasn't much she had to say to him that he actually wanted to hear.

On the television screen, Bill still stood before the bank of microphones and continued to explain in detail his plans for reallocating city funds. Eloise wasn't sure how much longer his speech would last. But he would take questions afterward, and then, if she were lucky, he'd go back to his office in city hall to field telephone calls.

"I have to go," she said to Allison, turning to make her way back to her office.

"Where?" her assistant asked, catching her by the arm and stopping her for a moment.

"City Hall. I have to…have to talk to Bill…um, Mayor Harper." She eased her arm free of Allison's hold and smiled reassuringly. "I'll be back as soon as I can. Hold down the fort for me in the meantime, okay?"

"Okay." Impulsively, Allison reached over and gave Eloise a hug. "We're going to be all right, aren't we?"

"Yes, we're most certainly going to be all right."

Hurrying down the hallway to her office to collect her coat and purse, Eloise knew that she had spoken the truth regarding Manhattan Multiples. As for herself, she wasn't so sure.

She had thought that losing Bill seventeen years ago had been devastating. But losing him again now, especially through her own foolish fault, would be even worse. She had recovered seventeen years ago, but she hadn't known then what she'd truly lost. Now she did, and she knew instinctively that she would never be the same again…ever.

Making her way to the lobby, somewhat distracted, Eloise heard a man's voice order loudly, "Don't move, any of you. I've got a gun and I'm not afraid to use it."

The sounds of a slight commotion followed, and someone let out a muffled cry of distress.

Snapped back to the moment at hand, Eloise paused in the hallway. She realized immediately what was happening. The man who had only threatened anonymously in the past had decided to show his face. He couldn't have chosen a better moment, either, since everyone's attention had been fixed on the television.

Quickly she pulled her cell phone from her purse and dialed 911, then calmly and quietly explained the situation to the operator who came on the line.

"Where is she?" the man shouted, his words sounding slightly slurred. "Where's that meddling old biddy, Eloise Vale? Thinks she can break up a man's family. Well, I'll show her—"

"Darren, stop being so foolish. Please put the gun down now."

Eloise recognized the surprisingly firm female voice that cut him off as that of Leah Simpson.

Setting her coat and purse on a chair in the hallway, then tucking her cell phone, still connected to the 911 operator, into the pocket of her black wool skirt, Eloise drew a steadying breath and continued down the hallway to the lobby. She didn't want anyone to get hurt, and it was her responsibility to protect her staff as best she could. She stepped into view of the gun-waving man and somehow managed to speak to him in a calm voice, belying her inner anxiety.

"I'm right here, Mr.—Simpson, is it?"

"Yeah, that's right. I'm Darren Simpson—husband of Leah Simpson. Who the hell are you?" he demanded.

"I'm Eloise Vale, director of Manhattan Multiples."

From the corner of her eye, she saw Tony Martino, the security guard, moving quietly into position behind Darren Simpson. But she held her gaze steady on Simpson as she added, "How can I help you, sir?"

"You can stop interfering with my wife, giving her ideas, making her think she can leave me."

"You're the one who left me, Darren," Leah reminded him.

"Had to. I couldn't stand all your whining about money to pay bills—"

With a leap, Tony Martino tackled Darren Simpson in midharangue. The gun flew from his hand and landed with an odd clatter on the floor near Eloise. She bent to pick it up, then smiled and shook her head. All that drama for nothing, she thought. The gun wasn't real, but rather a realistic looking toy made of plastic.

"I'm so sorry, Eloise," Leah Simpson said, the first of the staff to hurry over to her once Tony had the man facedown on the floor and locked securely into handcuffs.

"It's not your fault, Leah. It's his fault for being so stupid," Eloise assured the woman. "You were very brave. You don't have any reason to be ashamed."

She gave Leah a hug, then turned her attention to the police who had just arrived. They wasted no time hauling Darren off to jail, and once they were gone, Eloise made sure the rest of her staff was all right.

Though given a good scare, everyone recovered remarkably well in a very short time. Eloise was specially relieved that no one was injured in any way. She was glad, too, that the identity of their anonymous letter writer had finally been revealed, and that he wouldn't be making any more threats against Manhattan Multiples for a very long time to come. She also dismissed all praise for her bravery with a wave of her hand.

"Just part of my job," she quipped, relieved that no one had noticed just how frightened she'd been.

Everyone was okay and nothing else really mattered—except getting to city hall. The mayor had concluded his press conference while she was still dealing with Darren Simpson, and a soap opera now played on the television screen.

Would she be too late to catch up with Bill? She had to at least try. She owed him so much and she intended to let him know it even if she had to camp outside his city hall office the rest of the day.

"Okay, I'm out of here," she said to Allison.

"Still going to city hall?"

"Yes, but I'll be back."

"Or not," Allison replied with a teasing grin.

"I could be so lucky. But I've blown it with Mayor Harper, no two ways about it."

"Maybe not." Allison gave her arm an encouraging squeeze. "Just be your usual sweet, irresistible self."

"As opposed to being a meddling old biddy?"

"Oh, Eloise, you're not old and you're certainly not a biddy," Allison chided.

"What about meddling?"

"Um, I think I'll have to take the Fifth on that question."

Eloise stared at her assistant in surprise.

"Me…meddling?"

"Go to city hall, Eloise, and thank the mayor for all of us."

"We're going to have a little talk when I get back."

"Okay, okay…now go."

She wasn't meddling. Was she? She never meddled. Did she? Well, maybe just a little…occasionally…for a good cause.

On the sidewalk Eloise hailed a taxi and, once inside, set aside all thoughts except those of how best to tell Bill how sorry she was for being almost as stupid as Darren Simpson.

"This just in from our news room," came the voice of the news anchor on the local network station tuned in on the television in Bill's city hall office.

He and Wally had been watching the noon newscast to see how his speech at the press conference was being reported as well as received. The consensus was quite well on both counts.

"An armed gunman was arrested almost an hour ago at the office of Manhattan Multiples. Darren Simpson, the estranged husband of employee Leah Simpson entered the lobby waving a gun and demanding to see Eloise Vale. Ms. Vale—"

Bill stood, walked quickly to the coatrack and grabbed his overcoat, the rest of the news bulletin nothing more than white noise in the background. All he could think of was Eloise, squaring off with a man with a gun. The news anchor had said no one was injured in the scuffle, but she must have been terrified.

He had to see for himself that she was all right. Had to hold her in his arms and sooth away whatever fears she had.

"Where are you going?" Wally asked.

"To Manhattan Multiples to make sure Eloise is all right."

"The news anchor said no one was injured."

"I heard him, Wally. But I'm still going over there."

"Might not be a good idea so soon after the press conference. There were still a few mutterings of favoritism to be heard after your speech," Wally pointed out.

"To hell with that. All I care about right now is Eloise." Turning away from his chief of staff, Bill strode purposefully to his office doorway. "Call my driver and have him waiting at the curb in my limousine."

"When will you be back?"

"Maybe never," Bill replied, then smiled as he glimpsed the horrified look on Wally's face.

The elevator seemed to take forever. Bill had a hard time standing still and appearing complacent, but it was either that or stir interest among the other people milling around the hallway.

The elevator that finally arrived was the one directly in front of Bill. The doors opened and only one person stood inside the car—Eloise Vale. She met his gaze, her eyes wide and wary.

He stepped onto the elevator without hesitation, using his body to block the entry so no one else could join them before the doors closed again. Once they were alone, he reached over wordlessly and pushed the stop button. Then he took a step forward, put his hands on her shoulders and pulled her close for a long, hard kiss.

Finally allowed to come up for air, Eloise blinked her eyes as she looked up at him again.

"Does that mean you forgive me?" she asked after a moment, her hopeful voice barely above a whisper.

"No, it doesn't. It means I'm relieved that I didn't have to wait until I got to your office to find out that you're okay."

"You were on your way to Manhattan Multiples?"

"I saw the news report about the gunman who threatened you."

"He only had a toy gun," she explained. "I was never in any real danger."

"Thank God for that. Now why are *you* here?"

"I wanted to thank you personally for all the hard work you did to spare some city funds for Manhattan Multiples. Your solution to the problem was brilliant. I can't believe we didn't think of it sooner. It obviously took someone with true vision—"

"Flattery will get you nowhere," he warned in a stern tone of voice.

"I also wanted to apologize for the way I behaved last night. I should have trusted you enough to hear what you had to say instead of jumping to all the wrong conclusions."

"Yes, you should have."

"And I knew that if I didn't come to you, you'd never know how much I regret the things I said and did. Because you said you weren't coming back. But you *were* just now, weren't you?"

"Occasionally I make rash statements and jump to wrong conclusions, too. I thought I could put you out of my mind and out of my heart, especially after the way your treated me. I also thought I could stay away from you, but I can't. You mean too much to me, Eloise. But I do need you to trust me. I do need for you to believe that I will always have your best interests at heart and that you will always be the number-one priority in my life."

"I do trust you, Bill, with all my heart. I was hurt and upset last night, and I made a big mistake letting my emotions, confused as they were, get in the way of my deeper feeling for you. I love you, Bill, I love you so much." Hesitantly she reached out and touched his cheek. "Can you believe me?"

"Yes, I believe you. And I love you, too, more than anything."

He pulled her into his arms and kissed her again, taking his time, wanting her to feel just how much he cared for her.

"*That* means I forgive you," he said after a while, his voice husky. "Now I have a very important question to ask you. No need to hurry your answer, though. I want you to be completely sure before your make a commitment or not."

"Okay, ask me," she urged with a shy smile.

"Eloise Vale, love of my life, will you marry me?"

"Oh, yes," she replied without an instant's hesitation. "Oh, yes, I will marry you, Bill Harper."

Again he pulled her close for another deep, drugging kiss that lasted quite a while. Finally they were interrupted, rather rudely, by the pounding of fists on the elevator doors.

"Mayor Harper, are you in there?" Wally called out. "Rap twice on the door if you're okay. Otherwise I'm calling the rescue squad."

"Oh, hell…"

Turning away from Eloise, Bill gave the door two sharp raps, then released the stop button and hit the one marked *G* for the ground floor.

"Where are we going?" Eloise asked.

"For a ride in my limousine. We may not be able to fulfill your fantasy because of the security cameras that seem to be in every elevator on the face of the earth. But we can definitely have a go at my fantasy."

"And what fantasy would that be, Mayor Harper?" Eloise asked with a grin.

"The fantasy that starts in the very private back seat of a limousine."

"Why, Mayor Harper, how naughty you are."

"Oh, Ms. Vale, you have no idea…no idea at all."

Epilogue

"It says here that 'the bride looked pretty in pink,'" Eloise read from the New Year's Day edition of the *Daily Express*. "Obviously written by a man."

Alone with Bill at his Hamptons cottage, curled up in bed, a fire crackling in the fireplace, Eloise continued reading aloud the details of their wedding the previous afternoon at Gracie Mansion. The affair had been very small and very private. Charles Goodwin had been the only member of the press invited, and he had done his best to describe the occasion in print.

"'The mayor wore a black tuxedo as did the bride's three sons who also gave her away. Wally Phillips, Mayor Harper's chief of staff, served as his best man. Allison Baker Perez, Ms. Vale's assistant, was her matron of honor.'

"Sounds rather spare," Bill commented, trailing a line of kisses across Eloise's shoulders.

"Like I said, written by a man."

"I hope the ceremony wasn't too…minimalist."

"The ceremony was exactly what I wanted," Eloise assured him. "I didn't want our wedding to be a political or even a social affair. I wanted it to be very private and very personal, and that's just what it was."

They had wed in a simple ceremony presided over by a judge who had long been a friend and supporter of Bill's. The only guests in attendance had been Allison and Jorge, Wally and the young woman he'd recently begun dating and, of course, her beloved sons. Charles Goodwin and his wife had been included only so that the occasion would be reported accurately in at least one newspaper.

They'd had dinner after the ceremony, then the boys had gone back to Eloise's apartment with Allison and Jorge who had offered to kid sit so she and Bill could honeymoon for a few days.

"'…at an undisclosed location,'" she finished reading.

They had agreed that the only place they wanted to go was the cottage. And Eloise deemed it perfect from the moment they'd toasted each other with champagne at midnight last night until that afternoon when they were still in bed, the papers, delivered by Bill's caretaker earlier, spread out all around them.

"So, Mrs. Harper, we've been awfully lazy so far today. Feel like a walk on the beach?"

"Maybe later, Mayor Harper." Tossing the paper aside, she snuggled under the bedcovers again and pulled him close. "Right now I want you right here, and I want you all to myself."

"My sentiments exactly."

Holding her close in his arms, he kissed her gently then none too gently as the love they felt for each other made them one in a way they had once believed would never be possible.

* * * * *

Don't miss an exciting new series from

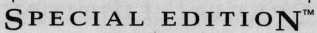

SPECIAL EDITION™

MANHATTAN MULTIPLES
So many babies in the big city!

With five very special love stories:

And Babies Make Four
by MARIE FERRARELLA
Available July 2003 (SE #1551)

The Fertility Factor
by JENNIFER MIKELS
Available August 2003 (SE #1559)

His Pretend Fiancée
by VICTORIA PADE
Available September 2003 (SE #1564)

Practice Makes Pregnant
by LOIS FAYE DYER
Available October 2003 (SE #1569)

Prince of the City
by NIKKI BENJAMIN
Available November 2003 (SE #1575)

Available at your favorite retail outlet.

Where love comes alive™

SPECIAL EDITION™

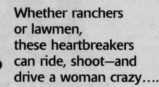

Whether ranchers or lawmen, these heartbreakers can ride, shoot—and drive a woman crazy....

Men are like chocolates—they are sinfully delectable and head straight for your hips! And Stella Bagwell treats you with Special Edition stories of devilishly handsome men to drool over—again and again!

Read all about lawman and single dad Jess—and the woman he let get away—in **SHOULD HAVE BEEN HER CHILD** (Silhouette Special Edition #1570, October 2003)

Then investigate rancher Ross—accused of a crime he didn't commit—and his lady lawyer in **HIS DEFENDER** (Silhouette Special Edition #1582, December 2003)

And look for Texas Ranger Seth's story, coming in the fall of 2004!

Available at your favorite retail outlet.

✂

Your opinion is important to us! Please take a few moments to share your thoughts with us about your experiences with Harlequin and Silhouette books. Your comments will be very useful in ensuring that we deliver books you love to read.
Please take a few minutes to complete the questionnaire, then send it to us at the address below.

Send your completed questionnaires to:
Harlequin/Silhouette Reader Survey, P.O. Box 9046, Buffalo, NY 14269-9046

1. As you may know, there are many different lines under the Harlequin and Silhouette brands. Each of the lines is listed below. Please check the box that most represents your reading habit for each line.

Line	Currently read this line	Do not read this line	Not sure if I read this line
Harlequin American Romance	❏	❏	❏
Harlequin Duets	❏	❏	❏
Harlequin Romance	❏	❏	❏
Harlequin Historicals	❏	❏	❏
Harlequin Superromance	❏	❏	❏
Harlequin Intrigue	❏	❏	❏
Harlequin Presents	❏	❏	❏
Harlequin Temptation	❏	❏	❏
Harlequin Blaze	❏	❏	❏
Silhouette Special Edition	❏	❏	❏
Silhouette Romance	❏	❏	❏
Silhouette Intimate Moments	❏	❏	❏
Silhouette Desire	❏	❏	❏

2. Which of the following best describes why you bought *this book?* One answer only, please.

the picture on the cover	❏	the title	❏
the author	❏	the line is one I read often	❏
part of a miniseries	❏	saw an ad in another book	❏
saw an ad in a magazine/newsletter	❏	a friend told me about it	❏
I borrowed/was given this book	❏	other: _____	❏

3. Where did you buy *this book?* One answer only, please.

at Barnes & Noble	❏	at a grocery store	❏
at Waldenbooks	❏	at a drugstore	❏
at Borders	❏	on eHarlequin.com Web site	❏
at another bookstore	❏	from another Web site	❏
at Wal-Mart	❏	Harlequin/Silhouette Reader	❏
at Target	❏	Service/through the mail	
at Kmart	❏	used books from anywhere	❏
at another department store or mass merchandiser	❏	I borrowed/was given this book	❏

4. On average, how many Harlequin and Silhouette books do you buy at one time?

I buy _____ books at one time	❏
I rarely buy a book	❏

MRQ403SSE-1A

5. How many times per month do you shop for any *Harlequin and/or Silhouette* books?
One answer only, please.

1 or more times a week	❏	a few times per year	❏
1 to 3 times per month	❏	less often than once a year	❏
1 to 2 times every 3 months	❏	never	❏

6. When you think of your ideal heroine, which *one* statement describes her the best?
One answer only, please.

She's a woman who is strong-willed	❏	She's a desirable woman	❏
She's a woman who is needed by others	❏	She's a powerful woman	❏
She's a woman who is taken care of	❏	She's a passionate woman	❏
She's an adventurous woman	❏	She's a sensitive woman	❏

7. The following statements describe types or genres of books that you may be
interested in reading. Pick *up to 2 types* of books that you are most interested in.

I like to read about truly romantic relationships	❏
I like to read stories that are sexy romances	❏
I like to read romantic comedies	❏
I like to read a romantic mystery/suspense	❏
I like to read about romantic adventures	❏
I like to read romance stories that involve family	❏
I like to read about a romance in times or places that I have never seen	❏
Other: _____	❏

*The following questions help us to group your answers with those readers who are
similar to you. Your answers will remain confidential.*

8. Please record your year of birth below.
19 _____

9. What is your marital status?

single ❏   married ❏   common-law ❏   widowed ❏
divorced/separated ❏

10. Do you have children 18 years of age or younger currently living at home?

yes ❏   no ❏

11. Which of the following best describes your employment status?

employed full-time or part-time ❏   homemaker ❏   student ❏
retired ❏   unemployed ❏

12. Do you have access to the Internet from either home or work?
yes ❏   no ❏

13. Have you ever visited eHarlequin.com?
yes ❏   no ❏

14. What state do you live in?
_____

15. Are you a member of Harlequin/Silhouette Reader Service?
yes ❏   Account # _____   no ❏   MRQ403SSE-1B

If you enjoyed what you just read,
then we've got an offer you can't resist!

Take 2 bestselling
love stories FREE!
Plus get a FREE surprise gift!

Clip this page and mail it to Silhouette Reader Service™

IN U.S.A.
3010 Walden Ave.
P.O. Box 1867
Buffalo, N.Y. 14240-1867

IN CANADA
P.O. Box 609
Fort Erie, Ontario
L2A 5X3

YES! Please send me 2 free Silhouette Special Edition® novels and my free surprise gift. After receiving them, if I don't wish to receive anymore, I can return the shipping statement marked cancel. If I don't cancel, I will receive 6 brand-new novels every month, before they're available in stores! In the U.S.A., bill me at the bargain price of $3.99 plus 25¢ shipping and handling per book and applicable sales tax, if any*. In Canada, bill me at the bargain price of $4.74 plus 25¢ shipping and handling per book and applicable taxes**. That's the complete price and a savings of at least 10% off the cover prices—what a great deal! I understand that accepting the 2 free books and gift places me under no obligation ever to buy any books. I can always return a shipment and cancel at any time. Even if I never buy another book from Silhouette, the 2 free books and gift are mine to keep forever.

235 SDN DNUR
335 SDN DNUS

Name	(PLEASE PRINT)
Address	Apt.#
City	State/Prov.	Zip/Postal Code

* Terms and prices subject to change without notice. Sales tax applicable in N.Y.
** Canadian residents will be charged applicable provincial taxes and GST.
All orders subject to approval. Offer limited to one per household and not valid to current Silhouette Special Edition® subscribers.
® are registered trademarks of Harlequin Books S.A., used under license.

©1998 Harlequin Enterprises Limited

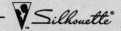

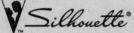
Silhouette®

COMING NEXT MONTH